THE REALITY GAME

··

Gisele Tumberg

Contents

Chapter 1

- -

As I awakened, I listened to the sounds around me.

The room was silent, except for my own breathing.

I was tired, but there was no way I would admit that to anyone. No matter how I felt, people around me would think I was fine.

I felt pretty good, despite being a little sweaty from the plastic mattress. I pulled my arms above my head and pointed my toes for a full-body stretch. I groaned as stiff muscles relaxed.

I sat up, noting that my abs protested a little. My legs crossed as I rolled my head around. No headache. Good.

My neck wasn't as stiff as it had been the last few days. The sore throat was gone.

Five weeks of breathing through a tube sucks.

I lay, eyes closed, breathing deeply, rolling my head in a circle, taking stock of the room.

The antiseptic smell of the hospital mixed with something else; a moment later, I recognized it as hospital oatmeal, cold by now, clumpy as usual. It would taste like glue.

I listened to people moving in the hallway, the squeak of a nurse's shoes, the fast click of high heels accompanied by a heavier stride, probably a man walking with a woman. Indistinct voices grew louder then faded as they passed.

I could hear the TV from a nearby room. Canned laughter from whatever was on filtered in.

The smell of coffee made my mouth water as someone in soft shoes walked past.

I wasn't allowed coffee yet; apparently, six weeks wasn't enough to get rid of that addiction.

I opened my eyes and glanced at the clock. It was five minutes to ten.

"Damn it!" I said, my hard won calm shattered.

I settled down for a few minutes more of sleep at eight. My five minutes turned to two hours.

My stomach growled. I glanced at the plastic tray with its tan cover and shuddered.

Nope. Not going to eat the oatmeal. I'd cajole my sister Molly into stopping at Mel's for an enormous burger with onion rings instead of that.

I pushed the rolling table over to the wall as I swung my legs over the edge of the bed. The linoleum was cold under my bare feet as I stood holding onto the bed rail for a moment until I got my balance.

I felt a cold draft up my back; the damned gown was open again. I grumbled as I walked on stiff legs to the tiny closet next to the bathroom door.

"You'll be back to normal in a few days." I said, "And now you're talking to yourself."

A minute later, I was in the bathroom, with the overnight bag Molly brought for me when I told her I was getting out.

I turned on the shower and looked at my reflection in the mirror.

I barely recognized the woman who stared back at me. Her hair, my hair, was a wreck, flattened black curls with one side obviously much shorter than the rest.

A large rough circle of black fuzz left a flat area on one side, I squinted at my reflection, hoping that might make the hair situation a little better. It did not.

Dark circles under darker brown eyes that looked abnormally large in my pallid face finished the not-so-pretty picture.

The bandages were gone, but I wasn't exactly at my best. I stuck my tongue out at my reflection while I wondered if shaving my head was the best fix for my hair.

Worrying about my hair kept me from thinking about why I was in this place.

"Don't think about it!" I shouted to the empty bathroom, as I leaned on the sink, using my arms to support myself, forehead pressed to the cool mirror for a long moment.

I stepped into the shower, turning my face to the stinging spray, grateful for good water pressure and plenty of hot water. I washed my hair with strawberry scented shampoo and turned the water off.

The shampoo bottle fell off the tiny shelf with a loud bang.

I backed into the corner as my heart began to race. A "bang" was the last sound I heard before waking up with a tube down my throat.

I began to tremble and cowered in the corner of the shower, sobbing raggedly, until it passed. I had learned the way to get through these episodes was to breathe deeply until they passed.

It took a while to get to a point where I could breathe deeply, but I did and eventually, I was back to something like normal.

Finally, I stood and faced the mirror, wiped my tear-stained face, and mentally added red-rimmed eyes to my "not a great look" inventory.

After I got myself together, I dressed in jeans and t-shirt from the bag, silently thanking Molly for not bringing me anything girly.

My sister was older than me by ten months and we had very different aesthetics, in that I had none, and she dressed like she was going to a party all the time.

I grabbed the socks and shoes and sat on the bed to wait for the doctor to set me free.

A few minutes later, a light knock on the doorframe made me jump. My mind had drifted again.

I turned and tried to look cooperative.

It was a stretch. Being cooperative has never been a feature of my personality.

Dr. Goran came in, looking pristine as always. The man never had a single hair out of place or a wrinkle in any part of his ensemble.

His pants didn't even wrinkle. Normally, that would annoy me, but he was the one who was going to spring me, so I let it go. This time.

"So, how are we feeling today?" he asked.

"I'm good, how about you?" I asked.

"Any headache?" He asked, ignoring my kind concern for his well-being.

"No. No headache today."

Nausea? Blurry vision?" he asked, tapping on his tablet.

"No, neither." I answered, impatiently. "When do I get to leave?"

He sighed as he ticked his points off on his fingers.

"You were shot in the head six weeks ago. You were clinically dead when you arrived at the ER."

He sighed dramatically before continuing. "You have been conscious for a grand total of eight days. Give yourself time to recover. Most people in your situation would be buried by now."

He gave me a humorless look.

"Well, I'm not dead." I stated, feeling a little defensive. "And I'm told you fixed my brain with your experimental thing."

He frowned at me, so I threw him a bone. "Yes, I know they're called something-cells that I can't recall right now, but I'm not the fancy brain doctor, so I don't need to know." I grabbed a fistful of the thin blanket on my bed and twisted it behind my back.

"I'm fine. The headaches are gone, I'm awake and according to the physical therapist, I'm back to near full function in every way." I grinned hopefully.

"Now, I want to get back to work and find the ass...um, individual who...." I trailed off as a flash of movement caught my eye.

A man in a long black coat glanced in, met my eyes, and moved on.

I gripped my handful of blanket tighter as I turned my gaze back to the doctor who had turned to look out the door just as the man moved out of sight.

"Wandering attention?" Dr. Goran asked with a raised brow.

"Sorry. I'll focus now." I answered.

"Eager to get back out there?" He smiled, showing perfect white teeth. "You know, you wouldn't have survived if you had been brought anywhere else."

"I know that." I didn't mention that I knew this because he reminded me every time he came to check on me. "Thanks for patching me up. I appreciate it. I like not being dead. Five stars, highly recommended!" I chuckled nervously and, with some effort, let go of the blanket.

"Now, I guess I just have to figure out how I'm going to pay for all of this. I'm pretty sure insurance doesn't cover it. They don't like experimental treatments."

"Your insurance didn't cover it. My grant did. You'll have to come in for weekly checkups for three months, monthly for a year, quarterly for another, and then annually for three. We went over this." He looked a little concerned. "Are you having memory problems?"

I thought about it before answering.

"No. I'm just excited about getting back to my life. I'm focused on that." I admitted in a deliberately calm tone.

He nodded and tapped a few more times on the tablet. "We will send you reminders. Please do not miss any of your scheduled appointments. It is vital that you report any changes or new symptoms."

"Your discharge packet should have included a list of indicators that require an immediate call to our nurse line." He finished with a little frown, as if he thought I might not follow the instructions.

He wasn't wrong, I thought as I stood for the physical tests he did every time he came in.

He stood in front of me and pulled out a tiny flashlight. I sat up straight and let him shine it into my eyes. It felt like the light was piercing my soul.

Too bright, too close. I could smell his spicy cologne and a whiff of sweat. It was vaguely nauseating.

"Good. Now, walk across the room and back for me."

I obediently walked to the door and back. Had I always been so sensitive to smells? I didn't think so.

"Wonderful! Looks fine." He nodded approvingly and tapped a few more times on the tablet, then turned his eyes back to me. "I just sent the release order. Who is coming to pick you up today?"

"My sister. She should be here soon." I answered, "When can I drive on my own?"

"You can drive any time, but it is policy that we can't release you without a driver. Please call the nurse when you are ready to leave. More hospital policy."

He reached out a hand and I shook it. It was warm and slightly moist.

"Good luck, Ms. Ryan. I will see you soon. Call this number if you have any issues or concerns. There is also an email which is monitored twenty-four hours a day." He set a business card on top of my paperwork, turned, and left the room.

I collapsed onto the bed, shaking. I wasn't sure why, but it felt like I was standing on the edge of a cliff. One wrong step and I'd be plummeting.

As I went through a short relaxation routine, my mind drifted to the question I had been avoiding for the past week.

Release the tension in your head and neck.

What made six weeks a reasonable recovery time for a gunshot to the brain?

Let your shoulders fall and relax.

Must be some cutting-edge medical stuff, because he was right, most people didn't come back from that, especially not so quickly.

Arms and hands limp, head down, resting. Deep breath. Hold for a count of three. Release.

It didn't matter, I told myself. I recovered and was going back to my life. How it worked didn't matter if I stayed on the right side of the dirt.

One more deep breath. Hold. Blow it out.

It wasn't a great answer, but it was all I had for the moment, and I had to be ready and, more important, acting like my old self when Molly showed up.

I might not be able to shake the feeling that something wasn't right, but until I had more information, being alive would have to be enough.

Fake it until you make it. Stupid saying, but it fit with where I was now. Something felt wrong, but I was breathing and functional, so I could put that on the back burner for a while, at least until I had privacy and my laptop.

I stood, opened my eyes, and bit off a scream when I saw that I was no longer alone.

A man in a long black coat stood in my room. I reflexively noted that he was a bit over six feet, fit, short black hair. Blue eyes. There was a small scar on the left side of his chin.

"Oh, jeez, you scared me!" I glared at him as I met his gaze.

His eyes were cold and lifeless as he stared at me.

I stared back.

Was he the man who glanced into the room while I was with the doctor?

"Are you lost? Didn't you pass by a little while ago?" I tried to keep my anxiety hidden. I breathed slowly, deliberately to hide the fear coursing through me.

He looked into my eyes.

I gazed back at him, maintaining eye contact, hoping he wasn't a violent psychopath.

There was nothing in the room to use as a weapon, except maybe my breakfast tray. I slid off the bed, putting it between the two of us and prepared to fight or run if I needed to, balancing my body so I could move quickly.

"You have no idea who I am, do you?"

His voice was quiet and steady. It sounded as if he was trying to be patient.

I recognize the tone. I hear it a lot.

If he was here to hurt me, he would have closed the door. Probably.

I choked back the urge to laugh hysterically and clenched my hand into a fist, fingernails digging into my palm.

Then I put my metaphorical big girl pants on and stared at him. Maybe we had met before. It was possible that I knew him.

Nothing.

I sighed and shook my head.

"No." I admitted "I saw you walk past the door a little while ago, but I don't know you. However, to be fair, I did get shot in the head recently." I chuckled nervously, holding my fear in fisted hands. "So, if I should know you, I have an excuse. I can even get a note from the doctor."

He didn't so much as crack a smile at my, admittedly feeble, attempt at humor.

"You will. I have to go now, but I will contact you again."

"Um, okay." I said, "Why? And I will what? Have we met before?"

"No, we haven't." He sighed. "You'll understand in the next few days."

With that bizarre pronouncement, he turned and walked out the door, turning the corner just as Molly swept in, looking fancy in a flowered dress, high heels, and a big smile. She was carrying a bouquet of shiny balloons.

"So, Mara, you ready to go home?" She beamed at me, and I couldn't help but grin back. I relaxed, seeing her familiar face.

I didn't need to concentrate on keeping calm with Molly, unless we were arguing and even then, it was familiar and comfortable.

She has always been a ray of sunshine, my opposite in every way. She caters weddings, I investigate cheating spouses for divorce lawyers. I am often rude and short with people; she is the kindest person I've ever known.

Her one flaw is that she thinks she can tell me what to do.

"I'm ready to go. But we're going to have a burger, then you can take me to the office." I dumped the pile of papers into the overnight bag.

"My new phone was shipped there, and I need to talk to Rick about what I missed. He can drop me at home later."

I stepped into the bathroom and tossed my small stash of toiletries into the bag only to turn and find Molly in the doorway looking impatient.

I felt lighter. Arguing with Molly was familiar; it did more for my mood than breathing exercises.

"I'm taking you to Mom and Dad's, so that they can keep an eye on you while you recover." Her tone and expression told me she wasn't going to back down, but I expected her to push back and had a counteroffer ready to go.

"First off, I don't need anyone to keep an eye on me! How about the burger then a stop at the office for mail and my phone first?"

I looked her right in the eye as I continued. "Maybe I should have called Rick, he would have let me do my own thing!" I knew that would get a rise out of her.

"Fine. Burger, office, home." Molly crossed her arms in front of her as she gave me her big sister look along with a heavy sigh. "And quit rolling your eyes at me! By the way, I called Rick and told him to call me if you tried to get him to take you home."

She smirked, knowing she had scored a point in our eternal battle.

"I don't live with them anymore, you know. I have my own place. But I guess it is home, sort of." I agreed, sulking because she was right. Being with Mom and Dad would be good.

Molly picked up my bag and handed me the balloons. I was happy she ignored the wheelchair and let me walk out, because I was prepared to fight her over that.

"Hey, aren't we supposed to get the nurse? I asked.

"I can break a rule now and then too." She answered with a toss of her hair. "I stopped by on my way in. I know you don't like feeling helpless."

As we walked out, I spied the stranger in the black coat sitting on a bench. He met my eyes and smiled.

I followed my sister, wondering what he thought was going to happen to me in the next few days.

His smile was not comforting. It almost looked like he felt sorry for me.

Chapter 2

An hour and a half later, we walked into the office I shared with Rick Garcia. We were partners in a small investigation firm.

It sounds more impressive than it is.

Our office is one end of a strip mall occupying two stores worth of space. There are three offices built into the space along with a conference room and a lunchroom. Our open reception area holds a couch, a couple of chairs and Kerry's desk.

The couch is comfortable and has colorful throw pillows that are soft enough to use for napping.

The other residents of the strip mall are a pawn shop, a decent Thai place, and a personal injury lawyer.

My business partner, Rick and I have been friends since middle school. The first time we met, we had a fist fight, which ended in a draw and a trip to the principal's office.

During two weeks of detention, we bonded over our mutual hatred of Algebra and have been close ever since.

We went through the police academy together and left the force together to work for Harry Carter, the previous occupant of the office, back when it was half the size it is now.

Four years later, we were on our own, with Harry's client list and a flourishing, profitable business.

Harry was happily retired and traveling the country with his wife, Sharon, in an enormous RV. I missed his dry commentary and sly sense of humor.

I walked in and waved at Kerry, our receptionist, researcher, file clerk, and gatekeeper. He was wearing a blue dress shirt that accentuated his bright blue eyes, which were fixed on the screen in front of him as his fingers flew over his keyboard.

"One black bean burger with onion rings." I said, cheerfully setting a takeout box on his desk. He gave me a nod and a smile as he continued to type.

"Thanks, Mara. Welcome back." He turned away from the screen long enough to reach for the box.

I opened Rick's door and noticed he was asleep, leaning back in his decrepit chair.

I dropped the to go box on the desk with a thump. He nearly fell out of his chair as I laughed. It felt good to laugh. The unease of being in the hospital was fading now that I was in familiar surroundings.

Molly and I sat in the two chairs facing his desk, I took the one with the mystery stain on the seat, while Molly got the one that wobbled.

"You know, that isn't funny." He said, chuckling as he pulled the box closer. He gave Molly a wave as he opened it to stuff still-warm fries into his mouth.

"Anything exciting come in?" I asked eagerly.

Molly gave Rick the 'don't encourage her' look.

"Mara, you just got back. Take it easy for a few days!" He picked up his burger, avoiding Molly's gaze as he continued. "Thanks for lunch. I left a couple of files on your desk. Nothing pressing, just a few insurance cases that need to be gone over so Kerry can submit them."

Insurance fraud was the second largest part of our business, right after divorce and cheating partners. Silver Moon investigations was on the top of the list for several expensive divorce lawyers.

I got shot while working one of the divorce cases.

We sat for a while, chatting, as Rick worked his way through his lunch.

Kerry and he had fielded all my calls and cases, so I was good to take time off. They both knew that wasn't likely, but it was thoughtful of them to give me the option.

I hated down time. I hadn't taken more than a long weekend in at least five years.

"Any word on finding the asshole who shot me?" I asked casually, leaning forward.

Rick looked past me and ran a hand through his short brown hair, making it stand on end. He did not want to have this conversation.

"What?" I asked, looking him straight in the eye.

"The case is listed as cold." His voice was monotone, and he clenched his jaw as he said it. That meant he disagreed with it but couldn't change it. In short, he was pissed off about the whole thing.

"It wasn't that long ago! How can it already be cold?" Outrage made my voice louder than intended.

"Mara, let it go for now." Molly said quietly, a hand on my shoulder.

I shook her hand off and glared at her before turning back to Rick as he continued.

"Detective Connor said there is no evidence. The bullet took them nowhere, gun wasn't found." He frowned and gestured to me to sit back.

I sat back, knowing that he wouldn't continue until I did.

"The guy you were taking pictures of was, um, busy at the time. His wife had no reason to want you dead. No one saw anything, and there is no camera in the alley." Rick's brown eyes sparked with anger.

"I kept arguing with them until Dave Shelby told me to leave it alone. Someone upstairs wants it to go away." His shoulders slumped. "I'm sorry Mara."

I closed my eyes as I tried to summon some inner calm. I drew in a deep breath and as I exhaled, I felt stabbing pain in my head.

Then, I saw a view of my own back as I watched myself take pictures through a motel window.

It was disorienting and unsettling to watch myself from that angle.

My vantage point grew closer. I saw myself, completely unaware, taking pictures through a window. A gun raised in front of me, in a man's gloved hands, in the gap between glove and cuff, a sliver of hairy arm showed.

I noted the suppressor on the barrel as I registered a muted explosion of sound. My body fell to the ground, as a pool of blood spread around my head. I never saw it coming.

Suddenly, I was lying on the floor with Kerry beside me, holding a paper towel under my nose. He handed over the paper towel as soon as he saw my eyes open but kept me from sitting up too fast with a gentle hand on my shoulder.

He looked worried which, for him, was rare. Kerry was always composed.

Molly was yelling, obviously upset. Rick was trying to calm her. It wasn't going well.

"We're going back to the hospital, Mara!" Molly declared, loudly enough to make my aching head pound a little harder. "Don't make me call an ambulance!"

"NO!" I said, more forcefully than I'd meant to as I sat up. I felt Kerry's hand on my shoulder, lending support, which was good because I needed it.

"Molly, I'm fine." I said, wincing at how shaky my voice sounded. "Really. It's probably just being up and around again. Maybe I do need to rest."

I did feel weak, my head was about to explode, and there was a fifty-fifty chance I would be vomiting soon, but I wasn't about to share that with the class.

"MARA! You passed out! Your nose is bleeding."

Molly's panic was helping me stay centered. Yeah, I'm a terrible sister.

Rick looked concerned, but he came down on my side.

"Hey, Mol, how about you take her to your parents' and see if it happens again. Could be she really was just doing too much too fast. The nosebleed is most likely from her hitting the floor with her face." He smiled as he spoke, knowing that Molly was a sucker for his slightly crooked grin.

She nodded, her face tight. "I'm worried about you Mara. Let's go." She picked up her purse and reached a hand down to help me up. "I'll feel better when we get you settled."

I pulled myself off the floor and slouched in the chair, taking a few seconds to get myself together, under control, and for the room to stop spinning.

I was on the verge of a panic attack about the weird...vision? Hallucination? Whatever it was, it was freaking me out.

Naturally, I covered as best I could. I held the paper towel tight to my nose to hide my shaking hands and leaned forward until I could project confidence.

I don't think anyone bought it, but they all know me well enough not to comment.

After a minute or so, Rick gave me a hand up and walked us out to the car. He held my arm like a boy scout helping an old lady across the street.

I leaned on him more than I could ever admit to anyone as I shuffled along like that old lady. I was thankful that Molly brought her husband's gray sedan instead of the behemoth of an SUV she usually drove, since clambering up into that beast might be more than I could handle.

I wasn't okay, but the idea of going back to the hospital filled me with unreasonable dread. I listen to those feelings, especially when they tell me what I want to hear.

Kerry rushed out with my new phone and the files from my desk, packed neatly into a box.

He gave me a hug and whispered, "Your laptop is in the bottom, fully charged." Then he pulled the bloody paper towel out of my clawed grip, handed me a clean one and headed back inside.

"I need to find the guy who shot me." I whispered to Rick, who still stood next to the car, as I pushed the box down under my legs.

"Later. Get some rest, he'll still be out there tomorrow." he whispered, with a wary look at Molly.

"Glad you're back, partner, but you really should think about calling the doctor." He said loudly enough for Molly to hear.

That seemed to appease my sister who dropped into her seat and started the car.

Rick has always been good with Molly, but with five sisters of his own, he's had practice. "I'll stop by tomorrow." he whispered and closed the door.

Molly was silent as we pulled out of the lot and headed toward our parents' house.

I closed my eyes, leaned my head back, and tried to ignore the pain in my head.

I was worried, on the edge of another panic attack, and I knew Molly was just as distressed, so I turned on the radio after a few minutes of silence.

A pop song came on and we lost ourselves in singing along at the top of our lungs.

Sometimes, you just do what works.

Chapter 3

Molly told Mom and Dad about my episode at the office the second we walked into our parents' house.

"Squealer." I hissed at her with the meanest glare I could muster.

She ignored me.

Mom and Dad started fussing over me and I grumbled even though a part of me enjoyed it. It is good to have family.

I appreciate all of them as much as I love them. Mom, Dad, and Molly have always been there, even when they didn't understand what made me tick, which, so far, has been almost always.

If I didn't look so much like them, I'd think I was switched at birth. They all seem to be able to deal with anything life throws at them. I wish I had that trait.

While Molly was busy ratting me out, something hit me from behind.

It was Leo, my nephew, Molly's only child.

I fell dramatically on the couch, and he plopped down next to me. Leo is five years old and my biggest fan. I'm a big fan of his too.

He's a great kid who will eventually give Molly fits, since he's a lot like me. He vacillates wildly between worrying about everything and charging ahead without a thought for consequences. He also shares my unruly, curly black hair.

According to my mother, he's just like I was at his age.

I'm going to enjoy his teenage years much more than his mother will.

As Leo eagerly shared the trials and tribulations of kindergarten, my mother handed me a blanket and a glass of water.

I must have fallen asleep on the couch because I woke up to the smell of meatloaf and fresh baked bread.

My stomach growled and I padded into the kitchen to investigate. I noticed as I walked in that mom had changed things. The kitchen island was now some kind of reddish stone, and everything was in different places.

I didn't like it. Home, in my mind should always look the same.

Molly was mashing potatoes and Mom was pulling a pan of golden-brown rolls out of the oven. An apple pie sat on another counter.

I took my usual place at the table. Conversation was light until my dad looked at me and said "Mara, when are you going back to work?"

Molly replied before I could even open my mouth. "Not any time soon, she has to take some time off to recover, Dad".

I glared at her. She ignored me.

"I plan to do some paperwork and some office stuff in the next few days, nothing physical." I assured him.

Molly looked like she might argue, but a hand on her arm from her husband, David coupled with a look from dad made her change course.

"Just take it easy, Mara. You aren't invincible." He said gently, before turning his attention to his dinner.

I planned to take it easy, but nothing ever seems to work out the way I think it will.

After Molly and her family left, I claimed exhaustion and went to my childhood bedroom.

The small, cluttered room still felt familiar years after I'd got my own apartment.

The walls were still painted the vibrant purple I had chosen the summer before I started high school, pictures were tacked on an enormous cork board on one wall, and a huge pile of stuffed animals watched over the room from a chair in the corner.

My bag and the box from work were sitting on the bed, so I grabbed the new phone and my laptop, which Kerry had thoughtfully put into the box.

In a few minutes, the laptop was booted up and the phone was downloading my old phone stuff from the cloud.

My phone had disappeared sometime between the alley and the hospital. It wasn't among my personal effects, so of course Kerry took care of getting me set up again.

I made a mental note that we should give him a raise.

I carried the laptop to the bed, with its bright purple and teal patterned comforter and lounged on the bed to do some research.

I typed in traumatic brain injuries.

After an hour, I came to two conclusions.

First, based on what I knew about my injury, I should be dead.

Second, if they had managed to save me, under normal circumstances, I would still be in a hospital, either comatose and never to wake up or unable to resume my life as it had been before.

Instead of being happy and relieved to be a one-in-a-million success story, I began searching for the name of the procedure on my discharge papers. It wasn't there.

There was little information about any of my treatment. The release paperwork was about care, future appointments, and things to look out for, rather than anything about exactly what had been done while saving my life.

I changed my search terms to find innovative treatments for brain injuries.

There was some information, but I had been led to believe that my injury was severe, too severe for even the newest treatments.

I got up and pulled a big, worn brown bear out of the pile of stuffed animals and sat him on the bed next to the laptop. He fell right over, so I propped him up again, before going back to my searching.

A lot of it was in medical terminology I didn't understand along with scholarly pieces that were far beyond my ability to understand.

Internet research is hit or miss on a good day, and I am not a doctor, but something felt off.

I reached up and felt the mostly bare patch on my head. The stitches were gone; the skin had healed while I was unconscious, and my hair was beginning to grow back.

I traced the scar tissue, an irregular blotch of skin with a line through it, where they had cut more deeply to get at my brain and wondered if I was being too dramatic about this.

Maybe the injury was simply less severe than I thought, and I was the lucky survivor of a moderately damaging bullet to the brain.

I should be grateful to be alive.

I was grateful to be alive, but I had questions.

I wasn't making any headway, so I put the laptop on the desk and plugged it in before I gave in to the exhaustion I would die before admitting to and turned out the lights.

I drifted off to the familiar sound of the wind in the trees outside my window, bear clutched close to my chest.

I was in a forest. It was dark, late at night. The trees above blocked out any moonlight, yet I could see a path stretching out in front of me.

The air was chilly.

I heard water lapping on distant rocks. It grew louder as I moved silently through the darkness.

I saw light through the trees and moved toward it. It felt like I was floating rather than walking.

I felt less anxious than I had in a long time.

At the edge of the lake a figure sat in a chair by a small fire. An empty chair sat on the other side of the fire.

The man from the hospital gestured to the empty chair. He wasn't wearing the black coat, he had on a blue and brown flannel shirt. I sat down and gazed into the fire.

"Do you know who I am?" he asked. His voice soft, almost gentle.

I stared at him.

"No. How I would possibly know that?" I answered, looking into the fire.

"Are you sure? Look into my eyes."

I met his eyes and found a name as I looked at his face. "Eric. How do I know that?".

He glanced at me then turned his attention to the fire.

He pushed a log with a poker until it sent a plume of orange sparks into the night sky.

"Where are we?" My voice was barely a whisper as I watched the sparks dissipate as they drifted into the night sky.

"Nowhere. This is a dream, Mara. Keep to the path, you'll find your answers. You might not like what you find, but you need to know." His voice was quiet and more than a little sad. "We both received a gift. Maybe it's a curse."

He met my eyes as he continued. "There are strings attached. Eventually, you'll have to figure out which strings you want to pull or be pulled by."

"We'll speak again when you know the rest of my name." He stood and turned toward the lake.

I woke in my dark room, with the sound of the trees rustling outside my window.

My heart was pounding, my body covered in sweat. It felt as if a cold hand was closed around my rapidly beating heart, squeezing it.

I had no idea why I was afraid, which made it worse. I could barely breathe as I lay, paralyzed by a dream.

"SNAP OUT OF IT!" I told myself.

The words, said aloud, startled me in the silent room.

I was angry that "Eric" had not bothered to give me any answers, just more questions. My rational mind reminded me that his name was probably not Eric, and a dream couldn't give me any information I didn't already have.

I decided it must be a strange dream because my brain was healing and creating new neural pathways or something. The guy in the black coat was just a convenient face to represent the unknown.

I obviously filled in the face of some random person who happened to walk past my door. Maybe I had dreamed him coming into the room and talking to me too.

Yes, it all made sense.

It made sense if I massaged it a little to fit with what I wanted to believe while still assuming I wasn't losing it.

I turned over and went back to sleep.

I didn't dream again.

Chapter 4

M orning came and in the light of day a sense of purpose. I would find out what was going on in my head.

First thing on the agenda: obtain a copy of my medical records, so that I could find someone to explain what was done and why.

I called the hospital and learned that I had to come in and request my files personally unless I was having them sent to a new doctor.

I put that on my to-do list, right after a trip to the office and before finding someone to make some sense of my hair.

My mother probably had a hair person, if not, Molly did. In any case, a baseball cap covered the worst of it. I scratched hair off my list and grabbed some clean clothes out of my bag.

Before I went downstairs in search of food, I checked the internet for stories of miraculous recoveries.

Now that was a rabbit hole. It was going to take some time to sort what might be partially true from what was obviously fantasy.

As I showered and dressed in the unintentionally retro bathroom between my and Molly's childhood bedrooms, I realized that I needed to find a neurologist to look at my file and tell me what they thought. I had no idea where to start on that one or what to look for in terms of qualifications.

I put "check with happy clients" on my list when I finished in the bathroom.

I had done work for several doctors and nurses over the years. One of them might be able to point me in the right direction to find someone to make sense of my brain.

Once I got that far, I'd need to find a way to get in the door without looking like one of those people with a conspiracy wall in my closet, covered in pictures, post-its, and yarn.

I wasn't quite there, not yet anyway, I thought as I wandered down the stairs and into the kitchen.

A note and a big tray of blueberry muffins sat on the counter. I grabbed a muffin and the note.

"Mara, Please don't drive yourself today. I know you plan to go out instead of resting. Please call a ride share or have someone drive you. I'm making lasagna for dinner. Yes, it is a bribe to get you to stay one more night. I love you. Mom."

She even put a little dinosaur sticker on the bottom of the note. Back in elementary school, she used to put stickers on our lunch bags every day, flowers for Molly, dinosaurs for me. I teared up a little as I ran my thumb over the colorful, smiling brontosaurus.

I put several muffins in a plastic container and called Rick. He didn't answer, so I left him a message requesting pick up service as I grabbed one and stuffed it into my mouth.

He called back as I finished my second cup of black coffee and first muffin while circling the kitchen island.

"Hey Rick, what's up?" I said, well, mumbled, my mouth was full.

"Not a lot. Want to ride along with me on an insurance fraud case? What are you eating? Did your mom make something?" He asked, eagerly.

I swallowed before answering. "Sure, if it gets me out for a while. Can we stop by the hospital after? I need a copy of my file. Oh, and yeah, she made muffins. Blueberry, with that crumbly topping you like."

"Job first then the hospital. No problem. I'll be there in about five minutes."

"You were already on your way here, weren't you?"

"I know you. Of course, you can't sit still for another day." He ended the call.

I chuckled as I added another muffin to the container. Rick had earned at least a couple of them for knowing me that well.

After a moment of consideration, I put the rest of them in the box. Stakeout snacks.

I knew Rick would have a thermos of coffee already, but I poured the last of Mom's into an insulated cup to take along. Caffeine makes the world go round.

Ten minutes later, we were on our way to check out Calvin James Malone. The insurance company thought he was exaggerating his back injury. He said he was completely disabled and unable to resume work. They didn't agree, but had no proof.

Our job was to find that proof one way or the other.

The companies were wrong as often as they were right, yet the invoices still got paid fraud or legit.

It wasn't the most exciting part of the job, but it paid the bills and destroyed any vestige of faith we had in humanity.

"Hey Rick!" I grinned at the vehicle he had chosen for the stakeout. "Ooh, suburban camouflage!" I said, referring to the gray minivan we used to blend in while staking out residential areas.

The baby seat behind the passenger seat was usually empty, but people pretty much ignore a minivan. Sometimes, in busy neighborhoods, we used a doll designed to look like a real kid, strapped in, as if asleep. No one wants to wake a sleeping child. I handed the box of pastry to Rick, put my coffee in the cupholder next to his, and wriggled around to find a comfortable position in the seat.

"Do you think I recovered faster than I probably should have, from this?" I asked, as I pointed to the side of my head.

"Well good morning to you too. And yes, maybe." He answered as he pulled out into the road.

His hands squeezed the steering wheel as his jaw tightened. He was grinding his teeth. He only did that when he was really stressed out.

Maybe I should start with something else, I thought. "Can you tell me what happened? I don't remember any of it." I asked.

He sighed and was silent for a moment. When he spoke, his voice was quiet, somber, eyes locked on the road, hands still gripping the wheel tightly.

"I called you because you missed a client meeting and didn't answer your phone. You never miss client meetings. Being late, on brand for you, but you always show up. After the third call, I used the FindMe app. You always answer, Mara." His voice hitched slightly.

"According to the app, you were still at the motel. Kerry had already rescheduled the client, so I went to see why it was taking so long. Figured maybe the guy had great stamina or you'd been made and run into trouble, like that time you got arrested as a peeper."

I chuckled and glanced at him. He wasn't smiling.

He was still staring at the road as if it was all that existed in the world. I breathed slowly, as I waited for him to continue.

"I went into the alley and saw you on the ground." I could hear the emotion in his voice, his eyes were wet. "There was so much blood, Mara. I thought you were dead. I checked you and got a pulse, slow, weak but it was there. I called 911 and tried to stop the bleeding."

I put my hand on his arm. As I touched him, I felt a wave of fear and sadness wash over me. It was gone as soon as I snatched my hand away.

I covered my quick movement by taking a big bite out of a muffin and handing him another one.

I knew Rick well enough to know he was troubled, I certainly knew how I would feel if he had been hurt, but in that moment, it felt like I was feeling his emotions.

That wasn't possible. The only explanation was that we knew each other so well.

"What next?" I asked after we finished our snack and got emotions under control.

"After the ambulance left, I looked around before the cops got there. Your phone was smashed on the ground, the camera was still there, where you dropped it, and that was it. There was so much blood."

He took a sip of coffee with a shaking hand. It was a long time before he spoke again.

"I thought you were going to die. I'm still surprised you didn't. However, you're incredibly stubborn so, of course you survived." He gave me a goofy smile, but his voice told a different story. "You even got enough evidence to get a nice settlement for our client."

"What? They gave you the SIM card from the camera?" I asked, emotional distress momentarily forgotten. "How'd you wrangle that?"

"Nope. Remember the argument we had about automatically up-loading from your camera to the cloud?" he smirked.

"Wait? It worked?" I was sincerely shocked.

"Yup, and there was enough there to make the case for the client. Everything until your phone got smashed was uploaded." Rick paused and stared at the road in front of us for a long time before continuing.

"To answer your question, yeah, I do think you recovered faster than anyone thought you would. The first doctor said there was no hope. I guess Dr. Goran is good." He didn't sound convinced.

"Who called Goran in?" I asked. "My family?"

"No." he answered thoughtfully. "He just showed up and said he was taking your case. He said he could save you and no one really thought about anything else."

"Have you checked him out?"

"I did a background check and some basic investigation. College then Med School, everything seems on the up and up until after he graduated. Then, he gets kicked from a residency, for reasons that are sealed for some reason." He took a big gulp of coffee before continuing. "No one was willing to talk about it."

"Wow. Usually someone is willing to talk." I commented. "If its sealed, someone always wants to spill."

"There's a seven-year gap before he starts up a private practice. There is no evidence of him completing either residency or any of the steps surgeons normally take. His CV said he did all of that overseas, but I can't verify any of it." He took a breath and held out his hand.

I dutifully put a muffin in it. "Something feels off about him."

He took a few bites as I sat and waited for him to start talking again.

"There's nothing on where he was during that gap. No social media, address, vehicle registration, nothing. No old girlfriends or boyfriends, parents haven't seen him since he left for college." He paused to make a turn.

"His mother asked me to tell her if I find anything. She hasn't even spoken to him since his third year of medical school. Said before that they were close, but in that third year, he moved and cut off contact with everyone from home."

I picked up the thermos and refilled our coffee cups, since both were empty.

"So, that five years. I can't find anything until he turns up with a private practice and privileges at several hospitals. He's on the board of Miracle Labs Pharma as well."

"Never heard of it." I looked out the window at the nice middle-class neighborhood we drove through. Mature trees, bikes in yards, just an ordinary place to raise a family.

"They've only been in business for a few years. Very limited distribution. They make expensive anti-aging treatments for rich people, near as I can tell. Exclusive and private." He snorted derisively.

"Why does a company like that have a practicing neurosurgeon on their board?" I mused, still staring out the window.

"No idea, but that's way above our pay grade or level of expertise. Anyway, you're here and in one piece. I'll take it." He stopped the car. "Ready for a fun-filled afternoon of waiting for someone to wreck his own life?"

"It's what I live for." I said, settling lower in the seat to wait.

"Me too, Mara, me too." Rick slouched down as well, a smile on his face.

"I'm glad you're back."

"I am too, Rick."

Chapter 5

- -

The site of the move was a blue split-level ranch on a quiet residential street. It was an old enough neighborhood to have mostly one car garages, which helped to make our van a little less visible. Newer and more affluent neighborhoods had fewer cars parked on the street, but the minivan went unnoticed in places where kids roamed the streets after school.

Rick had planted a few well-hidden cameras the day before during a casual early morning jog. We had a good view of the front of the house between the three cameras, so I could easily track what was happening from half a block away with my laptop.

Technology. It makes a lot of things easier, however being on site kept us from having to duplicate our efforts if something went wrong.

Our subject turned up about fifteen minutes after we arrived. Two hours later, we were bored, overheated, out of muffins, and down to the last swallow of coffee.

The man we were investigating walked slowly with a stiff-legged gait and hadn't lifted anything heavier than a couple of blankets all day. He sat in a chair, drinking cans of Red Bull most of the time, only rising occasionally.

I felt sorry for him. He looked like he was in a lot of pain.

"Let's give it another half hour then call it a day." Rick said as he yawned. "I'm going to the convenience store around the corner to get us some water and stretch my legs. You good here?"

"Yeah, I'm fine. Get me some gummy bears." I kept my eyes on images on my screen.

"What are you, ten?" He scoffed.

"Gummy. Bears. The regular ones, not sour." I turned from my task for long enough to stick my tongue out at him.

"Understood, boss." He said as he left, still chuckling about my snack food choices as if he had no questionable habits.

I turned back to the laptop with a smile. I was feeling much better now that I was out and working.

Spending time here, chatting with Rick, made a lot of the worry fade away. It was familiar, comfortable. Safe. It felt safe.

It felt like I wasn't losing my mind.

He had been gone for a few minutes when a red Nissan pulled up to the house.

A young woman with short blonde hair and an even shorter skirt got out and walked toward the house. She stopped to talk with a couple of the guys before the subject saw her.

When he did, he got out of his chair, ran to her, picked her up and spun around with her in his arms. They were both laughing, happy to see each other.

Happy or not, he was busted. He almost got me. I felt sorry for him for a while, but he was working the system. I marked the time stamp down on a post-it, so that we could find the footage easily.

I wondered where Rick was with my gummies and maybe some water.

The guy was walking around normally, talking with the girl, his back problem apparently completely healed. A miracle. Obviously.

I was disappointed. I really thought this guy was legit, but alas, no good guys to be found today.

As I waited, trusting the laptop to capture further evidence, my mind wandered to the guy at the hospital. Eric.

He said I would know more about him soon, then I saw him in a dream.

I was starting to feel something at the edge of my consciousness. He was familiar in some way, no, not familiar, but important.

I clenched my fist, welcoming the pain of my nails digging into my palm. It pulled me back to the real world, instead of whatever fantasy my injured brain had decided to inflict on me today.

I added finding a psychiatrist to my list. Maybe I was cracking up.

"Eric Michael Davis." I heard my voice say the words. Out loud. That was his name. "1438 West 14th Street."

I wrote it down and tore the sheet out of my notebook before stuffing it in my pocket. My heart was beating fast, and I felt another headache coming on.

Right after I dry swallowed two ibuprofen tablets, Rick came back and tossed a packet of off-brand gummy bears in my lap. "That was all they had. Are you OK? He peered down at me, "Got another headache?"

He dropped into his seat and handed me a bottle of water.

I gathered my mental resources and drained half of my water bottle. "Nah, just overheated. We need to get ourselves one of those vans with all the electronics in the back, then, we might be able to have some air conditioning while we do this. Maybe put a plumber logo on it or something."

Rick opened his own bottle of water. "That would be nice, but I think it still has to be running to have AC and a running vehicle draws attention."

He drank a little before sighing. "So, what's going on, Mara?"

"What? I'm...um, well, you see..." I trailed off under his level gaze.

"Seriously, we've been friends since we were thirteen. I know when something is bugging you. So, spill it." He looked hurt and a little annoyed. "You know you can tell me anything."

"I don't even know where to start." I bought some time by taking a sip of water.

"I think I'm losing it. I'm having delusions or hallucinations or something and I'm afraid to go back to the hospital!" I blurted out, the words tumbling over each other before I could stop them.

Rick reached out, gently took my hand and looked into my eyes.

"I won't make you go back there if you don't want to, but if that's happening, we need to find you help." He looked serious and concerned.

"May be PTSD. Remember how messed up I was after I got shot?" He twitched a little as he said it.

I think I did too, neither of us liked to remember that day.

I did remember, it was seared into my mind.

That was the day we learned one of our coworkers was working with a drug ring; someone we trusted nearly killed him that day.

It was the first and last time I ever shot another human being.

We both had problems afterward. Rick got help for his. I hid mine and worked it out myself by burying it.

It was what made us decide to take Harry up on his offer to let us come to work with him.

Neither of us had seen the signs at the time. We looked past behavior that, in retrospect, was suspicious. We ignored it because the guy was older, more experienced than we were, and we liked him. We trusted him.

I realized I needed to face whatever was going on this time, instead of pretending everything was normal. I could trust Rick with my life and with my possibly waning sanity.

"You're right. Maybe." I took another long drink from my water bottle, unable to look him in the eye.

"You can never admit to anything can you?" He said, chuckling. "At least I know you're not going to crack up right away, not if you can give me shit about it. Now, tell me about these hallucinations."

I told him about the man in the hospital and the dream. Then, I pulled the piece of paper out of my pocket and showed it to him.

"I wrote this down right after the guy over there...Oh, I totally forgot! You have GOT to look at this!" I rolled the video back to our money shot.

Rick watched with me and gave me a high five.

"Guess we're done here for today." He started the car. "Now where's that address?"

"What? Why?"

"The best way to find out if there's something else going on is to check out the address. So, we're going to do that." He put the address into his phone. A second later, a voice informed us that we were beginning the route.

Rick would stick with me, no matter what. I knew that. We always looked out for each other.

Chapter 6

The address I'd pulled out of thin air was on the other side of town, so I had some time. I suggested a stop for lunch, but Rick said no, not until afterward.

I slouched in my seat, sulking. Not my proudest moment, but I was facing a test. Either I was delusional or bizarre, impossible things were true.

Rick glanced at me occasionally as he drove but said nothing.

The silence was broken only by the sound of Rick's phone telling him which way to go.

Eventually, we turned onto West 14th Street. The neighborhood was old, with mature trees and neatly trimmed lawns. The houses were well cared for, the yards neat. It looked like my parents' neighborhood, solidly middle class, leaning toward upper middle class.

I sat up and looked at Rick. He slowed as we reached the address.

"GO! Just go! Get me the hell out of here!" I shouted when we arrived.

A man stood on the sidewalk in front of the house. It was Eric.

Rick stopped the car.

"Didn't you hear me?" I asked.

"Yeah, hard not to. I think you need to talk to him. I'll wait here unless you think he's dangerous."

"What?"

"Stop being a coward and go talk to him." Rick's voice was harsh.

I glared at him for a moment, then pulled on the door handle.

"I'm not a coward." I gritted out as I stepped outside. "I'm not."

I turned around and looked across a sidewalk square at Eric. He stood, hands in pockets, relaxed and smiling slightly.

"Eric Michael Adams" I said. "You said you could give me some answers once I knew your name."

He nodded, then walked toward the house. "Is your friend planning on waiting for you?" he asked.

"Well, he's my ride home, so yes."

I followed him up the stairs to the porch of his craftsman bungalow. It was painted a cheery yellow with white trim.

A small table had a pitcher of lemonade and a couple of glasses on it.

He sat in one chair leaving me to choose between the two others. I sat across from him and clutched the armrests with enough force to turn my knuckles white.

He poured each of us a glass of lemonade, then, he stood and looked around us.

"Mara Leighann Ryan. Miraculous survivor. Former police officer, currently private investigator. That's you."

"Sure, I guess. How did I know your name?"

"Your surgery. Look, it's hard to explain without a lot of technical jargon, but, the tissue you received helped you heal quickly and awakened latent abilities. You know how they say humans only use a small portion of their brains?"

"Yeah, I remember hearing that somewhere." I answered uncertainly.

"Well, your brain is learning to access more of its power." He paused to take a long drink before continuing. "The treatment you were given also adds some non-human cells."

"Wait! What?" I nearly started laughing. This had to be a joke.

"Non-human. It won't harm you directly, but you were chosen. I was too, the same way you were, with a bullet to the brain, ten years ago." He pulled his hair aside and turned his head to display a rough, round scar that looked like mine.

I stared, mouth open, heart thudding as I wondered if I was hallucinating.

"Chosen?" disbelief colored my tone.

"Sounds crazy, doesn't it? I didn't believe at first-" He cut off suddenly.

"Go to your friend's car. Get in and leave!" He stood. "NOW!" His face was an expressionless mask as he stood.

"What?" I stood, but I was getting angry, then I felt it. Not anxiety, but danger.

There was something coming. "Wait, I can help!"

"No, just go, please!" he opened the door to the house and reached in. "You aren't ready for this, and they don't know you've activated yet. It would be best if we could keep that a secret for a while longer."

He checked the shotgun he had grabbed from the house and put a hand on my shoulder to push me toward the sidewalk.

As he did, I felt surging anger with fear lurking behind.

It wasn't mine; it was his. There wasn't time to panic or wonder, the urge to leave overcame my disbelief.

"Find me afterward but go now." He gave me another shove, with a second dose of urgency.

I ran to the car and slid into my seat. "Drive. Get us out of here!" I told Rick.

We looked back and saw a black panel van with tinted windows pull to the curb in front of Eric's house. Several people in black emerged.

Two moved toward Eric's porch, while another team of two moved along opposite sides of the hedge line toward the back of the property. Two more stood on the sidewalk by the van.

Rick began to drive, obviously he had seen enough.

Everything inside me said to turn back and face them, but Eric had been insistent. I felt I should wait, and I knew I would be able to find him.

We turned a corner, and I couldn't see them anymore. I slumped in the seat, feeling drained.

"Mara, what's going on?" Rick interrupted my thoughts. "What's up with the van of goons?"

"Not a clue." I said, wondering how my voice sounded so much calmer than I felt. "I knew his name and address. He knew they were coming. How? None of it makes sense."

Rick was driving faster than usual, taking turns randomly, just in case we were being followed.

"Does how it works matter right now, Mara? Does not knowing change the facts as you know them?"

We pulled onto a busy road, a commercial area with lots of traffic.

"I guess not." I said quietly, looking behind us for the thousandth time. "Eric said something about me being activated, whatever the hell that means. He said I will be able to find him later. He seemed awfully sure of that."

Rick nodded. "Then, I guess we'll find him. Later. Hey, remember that Ouija board incident when we were in 9th grade?"

"Yeah. What does that have to do with anything?" My heart was racing. I was breathing deeply in an attempt to slow it down.

"This is creepier. So, what's our next step? You know I'm not going to let you deal with this on your own."

"Let's hit the hospital. I really need to have a look at my records."

Rick nodded and hit the turn signal. "We'll be there in ten."

I needed answers and I would move mountains to find them.

Chapter 7

Three hours later, I was exhausted, hungry, and more than a little irritable as we arrived back at the office.

The hospital was a bust. My physical records had been "misfiled", and the system was down so no one could access them. I spent nearly an hour waiting and trying not to lose my mind.

Finally, I got tired of waiting for something that would never happen and decided to go another way. Sara Cole, a former client, worked in the records department.

I jotted down a reminder to give her a call. Rick rolled his eyes as I wrote it down. He keeps all of his stuff on his phone, but I like the act of putting a pen to paper and writing. A list on a notepad is just satisfying. Crossing things off even more so.

While I was trying to keep from strangling the records clerk, Rick was working his little network of former cops and other useful people. He has better social skills than I do, so he has contacts in different places than I do.

Me? I talk to people who work on streetcorners, those without homes, or with jobs that make them invisible to most people. They seem to like me, probably because I just talk to them.

We compared notes on the way back to the office.

Rick scowled when I told him about the records debacle but reminded me it probably wasn't the clerk's fault. Chances were that whoever was jerking me around was higher up in whatever food chain we were looking at. The other option was that it really was just an error.

Neither of us thought it was a mistake, but stranger things have happened. Recently. Pretty much nonstop since I was shot.

Rick reached out to a desk Sargent. There had been no calls in Eric's neighborhood in the last 48 hours. While we knew the black van people weren't cops, no one had called in a disturbance, so no shots had been fired. Neighborhood like that, someone would have called.

Eric had either gone willingly or had been taken without managing to fire a shot.

Kerry was running a background check on Eric now that we had a full name and address. The report would be ready in the morning according to the text he sent me.

A quick call to the office reminded us that Kerry handles nearly everything; he didn't need either of us for anything.

Rick pulled up in front of my apartment building. "I thought you might like to get some more clothes and stuff before I take you back to your mom's."

"Thanks, Rick." I opened the door and stepped out. "C'mon in. I think I have some beer in the fridge."

"Sounds good. Hey, did you say your mom is making lasagna tonight?" He held the glass door the lobby open.

My apartment is on the third floor of a basic, aggressively generic building. Each apartment has the same floor plan and a tiny balcony that isn't big enough for anything but a plant or two. I started with four plants, now I have desiccated sticks in pots. I tried and I still feel guilty for killing the poor things.

As we walked up the stairs, I chuckled. "Yes. She even admitted it was a bribe. I expect she's already got a place set for you. She knows you almost as well as she does me."

"Yeah, but my mom knows you the same way. You know she had her whole church praying for you while you were in the hospital." He shook his head. "She's sure that's why you recovered so quickly."

I unlocked my door and we stepped inside. I sighed deeply, happy to be in my own space then collapsed onto my bright purple velveteen couch.

My home is filled with color, including the illicit turquoise paint on the walls. The manager doesn't need to know about that.

The furniture came mostly from my grandmother's house.

Grandma was what some people call a free spirit. My mother said she was a crazy old hippy. Whatever she was, I loved her and adopted her furniture when she passed.

It suits me, with all sorts of colors and textures and even more memories. An old curtain of beads separates the living room and the hallway that leads to two bedrooms and a bathroom.

Rick dropped onto the couch next to me, after a detour to the fridge for two bottles of beer.

We sat in comfortable silence for a while, until Rick spoke.

"So, what do you think you need to do to find this Eric guy?"

I thought for a few seconds, then shrugged. "I have no freaking idea. Maybe it will just come to me or something."

"Maybe you should try meditating. You know, sit quietly, and think of him. It might come to you." He said quietly. "We need some chips; I'll check the cupboard."

I sat up and stared at him. My mouth may or may not have hung open.

"What the actual fuck, Rick?" I nearly shouted as I stood and watched my best friend root through my kitchen cabinets.

"What? You don't want chips?" He asked.

"Yes, bring the chips, but dude, how are you so calm about this? I'm freaking out and you're all 'yeah, let's have a snack before you try to use your newly discovered mental powers to find some kidnapped guy you only met twice' like it's not abnormal?"

Rick sighed as he came back to the couch, wearing his look of long-suffering patience. He gets a lot of mileage out of that one.

I snatched the bag of potato chips from his hand and tore it open as he sat back down. He handed me a second bottle of beer and set his fresh one down on the coffee table.

"What am I supposed to do? Ok, Mara, this is strange. Beyond strange." He sat back down as he spoke. He was calm, like all of this was somehow not bizarre, his mouth turned up in a half smile.

"You think?" I said, rolling my eyes so hard it hurt.

"Before we moved here, I spent nearly every afternoon with my Nana. She took care of me from the time I was a baby, while my mom was at work." He shrugged as he spoke. "She watched shows about unusual stuff all the time. Ancient aliens, paranormal activity, alien abductions, psychics, the whole range of weirdness." He stopped to take a sip and devour a handful of chips.

"So, when I was ten, I asked her if she believed in all that stuff. She said she didn't know, but that it's good to keep an open mind and remember that there is more in the world than any of us can see. I know you don't lie to me, so the two possibilities are that you're having a psychotic break or it's real and we need to accept it." Rick leaned back and turned his head, so he was looking into my eyes.

"I don't think you're crazy, Mara, so this is me accepting what I don't understand." He shrugged again.

I smiled slowly at him and reached my hand out. He took it and squeezed lightly.

"Thanks. I don't deserve you." I whispered, feeling my eyes getting a little wet.

"Sure you do. I was afraid you were going to die Mara. That clarified some things for me." He paused, blushing just a little. "After we figure out what's going on in your brain, we're going to have to talk about feelings." He leaned his head back, eyes on the ceiling.

"Feelings? What kind of feelings?" I asked, my heart suddenly beating harder than it should be.

"Not now. There's plenty of time and you have some psychic shit to take care of. Plus, your mom made lasagna, so we should get going." Rick stood and took the bottles and chips back to my tiny, suspiciously neat kitchen leaving me to consider what he had said.

I must have misunderstoodbecause he couldn't have meant what it sounded like, but if he did, I wasn'tentirely opposed.

Chapter 8

After dinner with my parents, Rick went home with leftover lasagna and chocolate cake.

It would have been a fun evening, if not for Rick talking about feelings at my apartment. I hate talking about feelings. I never say the right thing and it's always awkward. Rick, however, didn't seem to notice anything abnormal. I talked with mom while he and dad talked about woodworking.

Well, to be fair, dad talked and Rick asked questions, because he seldom has time for hobbies.

When it was time for Rick to head home, I walked with him to the door. I was worried about awkwardness, but he just took his leftovers and reminded me to try meditating.

"If it doesn't work, we'll find him the old-fashioned way." He said as he began to walk toward his car. "Call me in the morning, either way." Then he climbed into the minivan and left.

I sat and watched a baking show with mom and dad for a while before I went to my room. I enjoyed the distraction as I sat between my parents, not thinking about anything beyond how good some of the baked goods looked.

Mom was enthralled and dad was more interested in it than I figured he'd be, but then, he loves mom, and cake.

After two episodes, I went to my room and sat at the desk. I opened my laptop and stared at the empty search bar.

I typed in "how to meditate", then backspaced over it.

I typed it again and deleted it again.

That wasn't doing any good, so I paced for a while.

Pacing? Not as helpful as you'd think.

Finally, I decided to go through some breathing exercises.

By the time I finished my usual routine, my heart rate was more normal, and my mind was clear. That said, I felt silly as I closed my eyes and thought about Eric.

I thought about the shape of his face, the color of his hair and eyes, his hands as he handed me the glass of lemonade on his porch. As I thought, more details came to mind, and I saw the scene at his house replay in my mind.

We were having lemonade and he started talking about my brain and what was going on in there, but just it started to get interesting he stopped and told me to leave. He reached inside his door and pulled out a shotgun.

What kind of people keep a shotgun that close to the door? That random thought nearly removed me from the scene, but somehow, I held on.

I saw the minivan as I walked toward it, well, ran really.

As I reached it, I felt something. It was the feeling when you know someone is watching you. I turned and saw only the van and black-clad people sneaking toward Eric's house. They weren't moving.

Nothing was moving. I saw a bird paused mid-flight. Somehow, I had pressed the pause button on my memory. Weird. Useful, but not normal.

I walked toward the van, no I didn't walk, I was just there. From the side of the van, I saw Eric standing on the porch, shotgun in hand. He was paused too. I was the only one moving.

I stared at him looking into his blue eyes and in the time it took to blink, the scenery changed.

It was jarring, but again, I held on. The truly strange thing was that I felt no fear, no anxiety. It felt kind of like watching a video clip. I was currently in "pause" and on to new footage.

The room looked like it was in a basement. A cement floor and small high windows gave that away. The room, which I assumed was part of a larger basement, had walls of ugly 1970's paneling. The faux wood made the room dark and shadowy; the only light was a single overhead bulb.

Eric sat in a sturdy metal chair, with thick zip ties on his arms and legs, fastening him to it. His face was bruised, with blood running down his chin, there was a cut on his forehead, and his hair was matted with dried blood.

He looked directly at me and smiled. His teeth were bloody. Gross.

He saw me, even in pause mode, he saw me. He didn't speak though, just the smile and then, back to pause. No time to figure out why that was, thinking too hard about it might toss me out and I'd have to start all over again.

Two of the goons from the van lurked in the room with Eric. I noted that neither wore the face coverings they had at Eric's house. One stood at a table, looking at an array of implements in a black roll pack laid out on the table, the other sat at the same table, reading a magazine.

Out of curiosity I glanced at it, "Birdwatching Quarterly". Apparently, this thug was a birdwatcher. I pulled my mind back to the task at hand with a little bit of difficulty and took a good look at their faces so that I could recognize them later.

Then, I glided past a washer and dryer, complete with a laundry basket on top of the dryer, toward the plain stairway and up, through the closed wooden door. The door opened into a tidy, spacious kitchen, with high end cabinets and marble countertops.

Another goon sat at the table, looking at his phone. I took a good look at him too. He was watching a video on his phone, not paying much attention to the world around him. Maybe he was on break or maybe he was the weak link.

The rest of the three-bedroom house was well appointed, obviously professionally decorated, but had a sterile feel, as if whoever owned it didn't really live there.

Nothing was out of place, not even in the insanely luxurious bathroom attached to the biggest bedroom. I couldn't see myself in the mirror in the bathroom, which reminded me that I wasn't there, not really. I held on to the thread of whatever I was doing, but just barely as I felt myself start to...fade, I guess.

I realized I had to really believe to make it all work, so I worked on that and in a few seconds, I was gliding through the front door. I took note of the house number, then glided around the house, doing reconnaissance.

Finally, I drifted to the corner to look at the street name.

I knew where Eric was being held. Maybe.

I knew that there were six men there, three awake, two more sleeping, one patrolling the perimeter of the property. I hadn't seen any security cameras, but that didn't mean they weren't there.

My eyes snapped open, suddenly I was back, lying on the bed, with an address in my mind and a massive headache.

I jumped up and grabbed my notepad out of my messenger bag to jot down the address. After that, I went into the bathroom to take some painkillers and splash cold water on my face. A line of scarlet blood traced down my face and neck from my nose. I scrubbed it off and decided to ignore it for the moment.

The clock said it was one-thirty AM. Well, that explained how tired I was, but I grabbed my phone and called Rick. If I was right, we would rescue Eric, or we'd end up in jail. It was entirely possible we'd end up in jail either way.

Rick answered just before the call went to voice mail.

"Mara?" his voice was rough, sleepy. "What time is it?"

"One-thirty. I did that meditation thing you suggested, and I think I know where Eric is." I pulled a black t-shirt over my head. "So, we need to go and scope it out."

"Sure. I need time to wake up. I can be there in forty-five minutes." I knew he was running his hand through his dark brown hair as he spoke, he always did that when he was tired.

I nodded, then remembered that he couldn't see me, so I said "Got it. I'll be ready. We should probably stop at the office. I don't want to do this without a vest."

"Good thinking. We'll probably need some other stuff from there too." I could hear him moving on the other end of the phone. "Just let me get some pants on and I'll be there. Make coffee. Bring it along."

"Rick, I...um" I started.

"If you're planning on telling me that you can do this without me, just stop. If I was where you are, I know for a fact that there is no way you'd let me go it alone." He sounded irritated. "So, knock it off. Now."

I let out a breath I didn't know I was holding. I had to offer him the out, but I was grateful that he turned it down. Not surprised, but grateful.

I finished dressing and went downstairs to figure out how my mother's new coffee maker worked.

Chapter 9

Rick arrived a few minutes after I poured the coffee into a thermos and two insulated cups and I ran out to the car, leaving a second pot of coffee brewing along with a note for mom in which I promised to take it easy.

I wasn't going to do that, but she'd feel better if I said I would.

Rick had his own car today, a sleek black Lexus sedan. I relaxed into the seat, enjoying the feel of the soft leather and the seat heater that he had thoughtfully turned on.

As soon as I buckled myself in, Rick turned toward the office.

I put the address into my phone and looked the property up on Google Earth. After a few moments, I realized the phone screen was too small. We'd look at it in the office on a larger screen.

"Looking at the overhead view?" Rick asked, having obviously consumed enough coffee to regain the power of coherent speech.

I nodded.

"I made some calls. Matt and Gia are going to meet us at the office." He continued, watching the road.

"How are we going to explain why we're doing this?" I was surprised and a little worried. They wouldn't understand all of this. I didn't understand and it was happening in my head!

"I told them that you tracked his phone, but that it's shut off now." He said grimly. "So, you said you have an idea of the floor plan and where the hostiles were earlier?"

"Yeah, I sketched it out. How do we do this without ending up arrested or dead?" I asked, my voice higher than usual. Stress does that to me.

"No idea" he said, as he pulled into his parking spot behind the office. "That's why I called in extra help."

Matt and Gia were old friends of Harry's. Matt possesses skills that fall into the 'I don't want to know where he learned that' category. He's the guy you want up front in any fight. Gia's skill set skirts the edges of legality.

Matt is well over six feet tall, broad shouldered, muscular, clean shaven, with a blonde crew cut. He's quiet and doesn't smile much. He seems to be in his mid-fifties.

Gia is a couple of years younger than Matt and is his opposite in every way. She cracks jokes and laughs often, she's just a hair over five feet tall and has long black hair that is usually in a thick braid. She can hold her own in a fight, but she prefers to use technology. She taught me to pick a lock, which has come in handy a time or three.

Both are generally willing to help when we need extra manpower, and they always work as a team.

I got out of the car and saw our friends melt out of the shadows. As usual, I hadn't even seen them.

We went into the office to plan. I booted up my desktop computer and pulled up the property we were interested in then we all gathered around to look it over.

An hour later, we had a plan. Well, we had an outline, but it was as good as we were likely to have.

Rick and I put on our vests and opened the gun safe. After we got everything situated, Matt came and adjusted our gear. We had learned to simply accept it, though it was annoying that we never got anything to his standard.

Rick nudged me as we sat together on a bench in the back.

"What?" I whispered.

"Try it. See if anything has changed." He murmured.

"I...you really believe in this?"

"I don't know. It's worth a try, right?"

"Fine. I'll try." I closed my eyes and thought of Eric.

I didn't see anything, but just as I was ready to give up, I heard a whisper in my head. "What?"

I thought back and I felt my lips moving. "Eric? It's Mara Ryan."

"I know. It is quiet here. I'm alone at the moment."

"We're on our way. Hold tight." I thought at him.

"After we get you, I need some explanation for...everything."

"Agreed."

The tentative connection faded. "He's alone in the basement now. Or I'm a crazy person hearing voices. Could go either way."

Rick chuckled, but I heard tension in the sound.

The van stopped and Gia opened the back doors. She fiddled with a large black suitcase and pulled out a small drone. A few minutes later it was flying, nearly silent, toward the house.

We had parked half a block away, to the rear of our area of interest.

It was just past four a.m., so we moved toward the fence encircling the house and yard. The yard was large with little cover, so we'd have to cross some open space. We were hopeful that the early hour and darkness would give us enough cover. Well, that and the one big tree in the center of the back yard.

Ideally, we'd be in and out before anyone even knew we were there. Realistically, none of us believed we'd be that lucky.

Once we reached the tall wooden privacy fence, we paused. Gia had set the drone to hover while we moved, so we waited for her to scope out the area.

None of the goons seemed to be outside, an SUV sat in the driveway, and no lights seemed to be on in the house, save for that single bulb in the basement.

The plan had Gia staying back and keeping watch from above with the drone.

Matt, Rick, and I would move in quietly from the back yard where I would stop behind the tree and keep my eyes peeled for movement while Rick and Matt entered through the mudroom. The basement door would only be a few feet away, in the kitchen.

Gia handed out earpieces that kept us in communication. At least if it all went to hell, we'd know.

At 4:15 we were ready to go. Matt loosened two of the boards in the fence with a power drill, providing a narrow gap where we could move the boards out of the way and slip through.

I made it to the tree and watched as the other two headed to the back door and to the mudroom.

I heard the click of a tool on the mudroom door and watched it swing open. The men disappeared into darkness.

This was not the kind of thing we did often. If we needed to check something out, we did it when no one was home. I was getting anxious again, I could feel my hands shaking.

Three things I can feel, I thought. Bark on the tree, light breeze in my face, and soft earth beneath my feet.

Three things I can see. House, rosebush in the back yard, light in the basement window.

My breathing returned to normal. I took a deep breath and was feeling like this might go well when I heard a shout from inside the house.

Rick's voice came over the link "Hey, buddy, calm down." A choking sound and a light thud followed his words, then a dragging sound.

"What's going on?" I hissed into the mic.

"Early riser. Wasn't alert enough to put up a fight." Rick replied.

Matt sounded annoyed as he whispered "Enough chatter, entering target area. Quiet."

I kept my eyes on the light in the basement window. So far so good. Eric would be out in a few minutes. Then, I had some questions for him.

I wished I could do the thing where I could see inside, but it would take my eyes off the rest of the area.

A light went on upstairs. Fuck.

I whispered that information to the others.

There was no way they'd get out of there before whoever turned on the light made it downstairs.

I had an idea, but it meant running. I hate running, always have. Even so, I ran to the corner of the house, then to the garage. I figured that the upstairs light had to be in one of the bedrooms, so I had a few extra seconds because everyone has to pee when they first wake up.

I made it to the garage side of the house without incident and pushed the gate open. It swung on well-oiled hinges, silently.

My goal was there. The big, shiny SUV, black, with a BMW logo on it. Expensive. Whoever was paying for this had deep pockets.

No movement out front, so I snapped open my baton and crouch-ran forward. I swung it into the side window of the behemoth in the driveway.

I evidently hit in the right spot because I was rewarded with a honking horn and flashing lights as I darted to the corner of the fence where I could see the front door. The door opened and one of the goons stepped out. He was followed by a second man. It was Dr. Goran.

What was he doing there? I felt sick and angry, so angry that it took all my self-control to avoid confronting him right then and there.

Over the coms I heard a scuffle; sounded like something hit the floor. I hustled back to the loose boards in the fence hoping everyone was okay. I pulled the boards apart just enough to see the door Matt and Rick had disappeared through only a few minutes before.

More lights were on in the house and there was shouting. Rick burst out of the door, half dragging Eric toward the fence. Matt followed, after a short pause at the door, walking backward, keeping an eye on the situation.

Just as Rick reached the tree, three men came around the side of the house and the mud room door opened. Another goon came through and ran at Matt.

I helped Rick get Eric through the fence and held the boards so he could get through as well.

Matt paused, holding his leg. The goon ran at him, a big knife held low.

As the distance between them closed, Matt made his move. He wasn't hurt; he was faking it! With a couple of well-placed blows, the goon's knife went flying into the distance and he ended up face down on the ground, stunned if not out cold.

Two of the other three had disappeared while I was distracted watching Matt, but the third ran directly toward him. He dived through the hole in the fence just as Gia pulled up.

We heard the guy smack into the fence as we all piled into the van.

Gia sped into Mr. Toad's Wild Ride. After a terrifying eternity, we screeched to a halt at the rear entrance of a nondescript two story cinderblock building amid a bunch of warehouses.

We followed Gia and Matt to the back door where she knocked. A tiny old woman in jeans, a sweatshirt and bright pink crocs with hair dyed to match opened the door with a glare.

Once she spotted Gia, her expression changed. She beamed and stepped aside to allow us to enter.

Matt and Rick carried a now-unconscious Eric into the building which turned out to be a small clinic. A veterinary clinic to be precise.

"So, girlie, what do you need today? The woman asked Gia. Her voice was rough with years of smoking.

Gia looked at Eric and back at the woman with an exasperated look. "Really, Lou? You gotta ask?"

"Fine. Get him in the back room and put him on the table. Your friends can wait out in the lobby. Shades are down, no one will see the light." She glanced at Gia. "Least it ain't you this time. Matt? Any holes in you today?"

Matt shook his head and said "No ma'am" as he passed her.

"Good to hear. I love you."

Once Eric was deposited on the stainless-steel table, Gia led us to another room, a small lobby with a reception desk an old sofa, a round table with several chairs and a couple of mismatched chairs. I dropped into one of the plastic chairs around the table.

"She's a vet? Can she deal with this?" I asked, dubiously.

"He's not shot, just got a beat down." Matt remarked as he sat across from me.

Rick and Gia took the two remaining seats at the table.

"I trust her. She's my aunt; my Ma's sister. She's an oddball, but she's good. She patches up people who don't want to risk hospitals and she's discreet."

"Well then, I guess we wait." Rick said as he looked around the room. "Dibs on the receptionist's chair, I think I can catch a nap there!

We chuckled wearily as wesettled in to wait.

Chapter 10

I woke in a puddle of drool with my head resting on the table. It wasn't a lot of saliva, but enough to be embarrassing. Ah well, at least I wasn't snoring like Rick, who was tilted back in the receptionist's chair, mouth wide open, feet on the desk.

Matt was stretched out on the couch, fast asleep. Someone had put a throw blanket over him. I didn't see Gia.

What woke me up was Lou opening the door.

"You must be Mara." She gestured for me to follow her. "He's awake and wants to see you. Before you ask, yeah, he'll be fine. They worked him over pretty good, had to stitch him up some. Nothin' time won't fix."

I stood up and joined her, with a glance at my sleeping companions as I left the room. Neither of them so much as stirred, of course, none of us were running on much sleep.

Lou opened the door. "Gia went to pick up some breakfast."

I nodded. As I stepped into the room, she laid a hand on my arm. "Get some sleep after this. You need it. I got a place if you need to lay low. Just lemme know."

Eric was sitting on the metal table, dressed in loose scrub pants. He had a shirt in his hand, and he was barefoot.

He looked better than last time I'd seen him, but he had been unconscious and bleeding, so there was a lot of room for improvement.

"Hi." He said, pulling on a blue t-shirt with "It was me, I let the dogs out" printed on the front.

I stood next to the exam table and looked him over.

"So, is it time to finish our talk? Or do you need more rest? Because, honestly, I would really like to know some things." I gave him a look that was meant to be stern but didn't quite do the job.

"Can you hand me my shoes?" He asked. "You found me. I knew you would."

I found the shoes in a corner, socks tucked neatly inside them, and handed them to him.

"Yeah, I did. Somehow, I seem to be psychic or something. Or this is all a major hallucination."

I began to pace. Now that he was found and things were calmer, I was having a hard time coming to grips with how this had all gone down.

"Don't worry, activation is...disorienting for most people."

"Disorienting? Really?" I scoffed, pausing my pacing to glare at him.

He smiled ruefully. "I know, it all seems impossible. Most people aren't self-aware as you were. Most times it is controlled, carefully. In many cases, the subjects aren't even aware of it."

"How could I not be aware of it?" I asked, settling into the folding chair.

"Let me start from the beginning. Did you have a DNA test done in the last five years?"

"No, why would I...wait, yes. My mom had us all do a test for some genealogy thing. They sent us a report. I didn't bother to look at it, since I don't really care about that stuff. Why does that matter?" I ended by taking a deep breath.

In through the nose, out through the mouth.

"Well, those tests are everywhere. Many people are taking them, and some groups use them to look for specific genetic markers. Even within a family, there are variations that make some people..." He trailed off as if he was looking for the right word. "Useful to various organizations."

"Useful? To what organizations. Is this government stuff? Do you need some tinfoil to make a hat?" I asked my questions quickly; I did not like where this was going.

He chuckled at the tin foil hat comment, not realizing I was serious. This was next-level crazy stuff. Of course, everything from the last couple of days was crazy. So, I clamped my mouth shut and listened.

"I took one of those DNA tests too, about ten years ago. My wife asked me to since I knew nothing about my family. So, I humored her." He smiled sadly at the mention of his wife. "Her name was Beth; she was a wonderful woman. She died a year later. Cancer."

"I'm sorry." He looked so sad that I felt terrible for wanting him to get to the point already.

"It was a long time ago." He wiped his eyes with his sleeve. "About two years after her death, I was leaving a bar and got jumped. I ended up needing brain surgery. Everyone told me I would have died if not for my brilliant surgeon." He had his socks on and reached for the first shoe.

"Soon after that, I began having dreams and hallucinations. Except they weren't a sign of me going over the edge." He finished tying his shoes and stood up, holding on to the edge of the table for balance. "Other strange things happened too, but I tried to pretend none of it was real."

Uh oh. Sounded familiar. "What kind of other things?"

"While fixing my car one day, I dropped a wrench, but then, it slapped right back into my hand." He let go of the edge of the table for a second, then grabbed it again. He raised his other hand and looked across the room.

A big plastic jar of bone shaped dog treats on a shelf rose an inch or so, then moved slowly through the air to his outstretched hand. He set them down on the table. "Telekinesis. I can speak to people in their dreams as well."

"This is too weird." I said, standing to pace. "That's impossible, I mean, how? What makes that possible?"

"I had the same questions, so I decided to look up an old friend, a professor of Neurology and a former surgeon. I went to him to ask him the same questions." He tried standing on his own again and failed.

"For crying out loud! Sit down." I nearly shouted as I pulled the folding chair to where he stood. "Sit in the chair and tell me what happened!"

He sat. I perched on the end of the table, waiting for him to continue. I felt hypocritical yelling at him for doing exactly what I would do in his situation, but I needed him functional, and I needed some answers.

He sighed. "So, my friend ran some tests and noticed that the brain tissue near the site of my surgery was different than he expected. He took a sample well, two samples, one from the site of the surgery, one from somewhere else." He winced at the memory. "It wasn't pleasant by the way."

He stopped talking. I wanted to push him, but I felt this was bringing up some stuff he didn't want to deal with. I recognize the look and I could feel his distress, permeating the space between the two of us. Sadness and guilt radiated from him.

I touched his arm and pulled back. It was the emotional equivalent of touching a hot stove.

"He called a few days later and asked me to meet him at a park near my home. It seemed odd to meet in the park. We usually met up at a bar or a diner to catch up.

I waited at the park, but he didn't show. When I got home, I turned on the TV and there was a news story about a hit and run. He was killed.

"It wasn't an accident, was it?" I asked, though I knew the answer.

He shook his head. "A week later, I got an envelope in the mail. My brain scans were there, along with the name and number of a doctor. The note was from him. He sent my sample to her, and she would be waiting for my call."

Eric stood up, less wobbly than he had been just a few minutes before. "He knew that he was in danger, at the end of the note, he wrote that people were following him."

"So, did you call the number?" I prodded, feeling like a jerk for pushing him.

"Yep. There was a lot of jargon, however she said that my DNA was being rewritten by the tissue used to save my life. I'm not fully human, but I'm not whatever it is that they used either. I'm a hybrid, she said. Apparently, she has developed new method of analysis."

It was my turn to sit down, so I did. I think my mouth hung open. I waited for the anxiety attack to commence.

It didn't happen. Odd.

"So, I should assume that my DNA is changing too?" I asked, curious.

"I felt your presence in that hospital room as I walked past. Knew your name. It has happened a few times in the last couple of years. Most of the people who get this procedure never know that anything has changed. A small percentage, like us, are aware of changes."

"You've said 'activated' before. Is this what you mean by that?"

He looked skyward, then looked at me. "Yes, and it's dangerous to the people behind this. They prefer to initiate activation."

I realized a second later that his lips hadn't moved. He had spoken into my mind. Freaky, but again, no panic, no anxiety, just a bizarre sense of acceptance, of calm.

The door opened and Rick's head poked through. His hair was sticking straight up on one side. "Gia's here with food. Come on and eat."

We followed him out.

In my head, I heard "We'll, talk more later."

"No, we can talk with the group. We can trust them."

I don't know if I said it out loud or not.

Chapter 11

O ver breakfast burritos and coffee, and a bright green smoothie for Matt, Eric gave us an abbreviated version of our conversation, leaving out the bit about not-human DNA, which made me happy. I wasn't ready to have that conversation just yet.

Next, we got into why he was there, and it was, well, a doozy as the old folks say.

Eric met each of our eyes in turn and took a deep breath. He didn't seem to know where to start either.

"Now, this is all going to sound, well, crazy. I know that and I need you all to just listen." He looked around the table.

Matt, Gia, and Rick looked like they were waiting for him to get on with it. Lou, well, she looked like she expected this to be entertaining.

"I am a member of an organization that works with non-traditional life variations. I'm not supposed to divulge any of this to outsiders, but I think you deserve an explanation, and you saved my ass, so I'm going to trust you. Please don't make me regret this."

Rick raised his hand. Eric nodded.

"So, what's a non-traditional life variation? What does that even mean? Is it aliens?" He looked hopeful. "Because I always thought there were aliens."

Gia and Matt snorted.

Eric gave him a level gaze and said "Yes, it includes life that doesn't originate on this planet. It also includes varieties of life that do originate here."

He was serious. Everyone was silent for a long moment.

Except for Rick who broke into a huge grin. "Aliens are real! I knew it!"

Lou broke the awkward silence. "You're one of those guys. OK. Do you know Billy Cameron?"

Eric turned toward her. "Yes, I know Billy. How do you know him?" he asked cautiously.

"I have a bunker under this place, from way back when everyone figured we'd get nuked, Billy uses it during the full moon." She smiled. "Yeah, I know about him, I've known him since he was five. He trusts me, I think I'm the only one around here who knows about, the thing."

Eric nodded and said, "Thanks for looking out for him, he's a good kid".

Gia stared at her aunt in disbelief. "What. The. Hell. Aunt Lou?"

Matt laughed, as if it were a joke and Rick, well, he didn't react at all. He was probably still thinking about the aliens.

Eric looked around the table and met everyone's eyes in turn.

"I know this is a lot and I've got to ask you to roll with it, because I need your help. I don't have time to get a full team together. I can get some backup, but it won't be enough."

Rick leaned forward, apparently done thinking about the aliens. "Enough for what?"

"We need to get into Miracle Labs." His face was serious.

"Why?" I looked at him curiously. "Don't they make moisturizers and stuff for rich women to keep looking like they're 20 forever through spa treatments?"

"Yes, but that is the public face of the company. You don't want to know where those products come from, by the way." He sighed. "Goran and the people he works for are working to make changes to the local population. It is probably a pilot program. Mara, you were part of it; otherwise, you wouldn't be sitting here."

Again, we all stared at him, waiting for him to continue. Gia and Matt looked confused and upset, Rick was still just sitting there as if this was a normal day and an ordinary conversation.

I felt calm, which was not normal. This should be freaking me out and yet, I felt okay.

"Eric?" I said, my voice sharper than intended.

He looked toward me but didn't meet my eyes. "Are you keeping me calm somehow?"

He looked at his hands instead of at me and I felt it, him, in my head. "Yes. I'm using our link to help you manage your stress."

"Knock it off. I can handle it." I said, out loud, teeth clenched. "Talking to me is one thing, altering my feelings is off limits. Period. Got it?"

There was a moment of silence as the others looked between us wondering what the hell I was talking about, but that passed quickly.

I felt him let go. I heard a small voice in my head say "I'm sorry. I thought it would help you."

The anxiety came back as a buzz in the back of my head. I welcomed the familiar feeling; it keeps me on my toes.

Yeah, I'm an odd duck, anxiety is comforting. It reminds me I'm alive.

We needed answers and we needed a plan.

Eric made a couple of calls on Lou's land line while we discussed what he had said. It sounded crazy, but none of us were ready to dismiss it.

Gia and Matt said they had seen plenty of bizarre things over the years and Rick? Well, he was in the second aliens were mentioned.

I was in because I knew there was something sketchy about Goran from the start. I don't know if it was my regular intuition or the alien brain stuff, but either way, I wasn't wrong about him.

Eric came back after a few minutes. "I have two coming in to help. They should be here by three, which means we'll have plenty of time to get into place before we go in at eight. That's when the labs close for the night."

"I had blueprints and a floor plan, but I doubt that's at my house anymore, so, we're going to rely on my memory."

Lou was working on a laptop. "Get someone to the county clerk's office and you can get a copy. Might not be perfect, I mean, my bomb shelter isn't on the one for this building, but it's a place to start. Ask for Sheila and she'll get them to you by closing today."

Gia looked at Matt, then they stood up together. "Why don't we go and get the plans. Shouldn't take more than a few hours. Hopefully less. Fill us in on the plan when we get back."

Eric nodded and handed them a piece of paper with something scrawled on it.

Once they were gone, I turned back to Eric.

"So, what was that about changes and a pilot plan?" I asked. "You said you could tell me what happened to me. Why I was shot. Usually, random street crime doesn't come with a suppressor."

Eric sat back. He looked tired. Normally, I'd feel a little sorry for him, but I wasn't in the mood to cut him any slack just yet.

Rick was listening intently. He reached for my hand under the table and, jeez, I took it and enjoyed the feel of him holding it.

Finally, Eric spoke again.

"I went to the alley and looked at the area. One of my, gifts is the ability to read some past events. That alley isn't used much, so I was able to get some of what happened. I was able to get a good look at the guy who shot you." Eric stood and began to pace.

"He had an earpiece and a Sabre tattoo on his neck, those tell me he works for Sabre Corp. They supply mercenaries to nearly every conflict on the planet, security details to dictators and despots, and they have a large stake in, you guessed it, MiracleLabs."

"Okay, but why me?" I asked, genuinely curious about that. "I'm a nobody."

"The DNA test your mom had you take. I had someone check it. That test was one of theirs. You must have markers they are looking for."

He wandered to the wall and leaned heavily against it. I noticed that his head wound was nearly healed already.

"What kind of markers? What does that even mean?" I asked. "Is that why my medical records aren't available?"

"Records, yes, that's why. Markers? Well, they are looking for people who are compatible with the cell lines. Most people don't end up knowing there's anything unusual in there. They just move on with their lives, happy in the knowledge that they didn't die, until they are activated."

Rick was now pacing too, but he stopped for a moment. "Activated?"

"Remember that guy who shot up the mall a few months ago?" Eric asked.

"Yeah, what was his name? Oh, Keaton, what was his last name, doesn't matter though. He killed a bunch of people. No history of violence, then he keeled over in his holding cell before trial."

Rick sat down next to me, he was agitated, I could feel it rolling off him in waves. Plus, he was bouncing his leg.

Lou still sat nearby, working on her laptop, glancing up occasionally, enjoying the show, I guess.

She spoke, filling the uncomfortable silence.

"So, according to my search here, there's been a serious increase in mass violence in the last three years in this part of the state. Bombers, shooters, and one guy who killed twelve people in a bar fight."

She looked curiously at Eric. "I remember that story, he wasn't even a big guy, and no one could remember him throwing a single punch."

Eric nodded. "Yeah, I remember. We went to check records and they were all missing. There was a lot of irregularity in the paperwork too."

I thought about it for a moment. "What's the goal though? I don't see how this is useful."

Rick nodded. "So, they were activated, I'm assuming remotely?"

"Yes." Eric replied. "As opposed to self-activated, like me and Mara."

"And self-activated means that the person is aware that there are changes?" I asked. "Is that why you stopped in my hospital room?"

"I heard about your attack through a source, so I came in while you were comatose. I felt it while you were out, so I came back later and saw you. I could feel your mind fighting your inclination to pretend everything was normal." He smiled.

Rick glanced at me, with a raised eyebrow before turning back to Eric. "Well, you got her pegged, that's for sure!"

I glared at him. He laughed. Idiot. "So, why did Goran nab you?"

"Because I have been finding self-activated people and helping them acclimate. That takes them out of his, and by extension, his employers' control. He doesn't like that he can't figure out where my information comes from."

I thought for a minute. "So, if they can make people do terrible things, it follows that they can make people do mundane things too. You talked about a pilot program. People tend to follow the crowd. If they get the right people to do certain things or believe certain things..." I trailed off.

Rick picked it right up. "They can push public opinion in any direction they want to. With the right people and message, they can run any agenda they choose."

"That's what my associates believe." Eric's tone was grim. "And I tend to agree with them. The management of Sabre plays the long game. My associates do as well."

Rick stood up and grabbed some paper from Lou's copier. "Draw out what you know about the place and let's start working on the plan to get inside and back out without ending up dead."

"Sounds good." Eric said as he began sketching the building out.

The two of them put their heads together.

I sat back and wondered if I should have let Eric keep calming me.

Then, I just concentrated on breathing, thinking that at least I had something real to be nervous about this time.

By noon, Gia and Matt were back with the blueprints, thanks to Lou's friend, Sheila and fifty bucks under the table.

Rick and Eric had been planning and plotting for a couple of hours by that time.

Eric had an idea of the outside security, but practically nothing about inside the building.

He kept telling us that he had someone who would be able to deal with it, but it seemed like a big hole in a plan that was already more holes than substance.

As Matt and Gia worked on the plan, with Lou adding commentary every so often, I remembered my mental tour of the house we rescued Eric from.

"I think I can get us an idea of security inside once we get there, like I did at the house." Everyone turned to look at me. I waved and sat back down.

We were all armed, but again, shooting people tends to be frowned on by law enforcement, and carries an emotional cost, so, we were hoping for a working stealth plan.

A few hours later, we had an outline that would probably work to get us to the building. We'd have to wing it after that.

None of us felt particularly comfortable with that, but it was all we had.

Lou offered us her living quarters to rest for a few hours while we waited for night and for Eric's backup to arrive. I fell asleep almost immediately upon hitting the soft leather couch in Lou's surprisingly well-appointed apartment.

Chapter 12

I woke at nearly midnight to find everyone else up and moving around.

There were four new people gathered around Lou's kitchen island with the rest of the crew.

I looked at the four newcomers. A woman, about my age, short red hair, athletic looking, wearing a black turtleneck and spandex leggings held out a hand. "I'm Susan, you must be Mara."

I shook her hand as she continued. "This is Shawn." She gestured to a Black man sitting at the counter, sipping from a mug. A tea ball sat on a saucer by his elbow.

"Hello." His voice was deep and resonant; his smile lit the entire room.

The third new person was a gangly kid who couldn't have been more than seventeen.

"I'm Billy." He said with a tremor in his voice. "I want to help, if I can."

The fourth was a tiny, waiflike woman, around Billy's age. She sat quietly on the couch, wearing a white dress with a blue sash. Her hair cascaded down around her pale face in auburn curls. She looked up and said "Hello. I am Calia. It is a pleasure to meet you."

I nodded. Eric came in and gestured to us all. "Come on downstairs and we can work more on the plan. We have more data than we did a few hours ago, but we're on the clock."

We trooped down the stairs to the reception area of the clinic and clustered around the table where Eric and Matt went over the plan.

Billy would fly Gia's drone to keep eyes on the path to a side entrance near the employee parking lot. It had the least lighting of any of the entrances, so Matt, Shawn, Susan, and Eric would enter there.

Gia and Rick would deal with the guard at the gate. From the guard post, Gia thought she might be able to get into the security system, if they were integrated. If not, they'd proceed to provide backup to Matt's group.

I would try to remotely view the place from a safe distance, while Calia, well, no one really said what she was going to do, but she nodded when Susan asked her if she was ready, so I didn't ask the thousand questions that piled up in my mind.

Susan pointed to two rooms on the map. "These are our targets, the file room, and the main lab sample storage room. Mara, while we're getting into position, it would be great if you could peek inside.

She was awfully calm about me being able to look inside places with my mind. I wasn't calm about that, it was freaky and weird and all kinds of wrong, but I played it cool, in my awkward way. I might have said "groovy".

Then, she went on for a while about how the samples were stored and other stuff that wasn't my part of the plan.

Before long, it was time to move out. We were planning to hit the place at around 3 am, when the guards might be a little sleepy and hopefully, slightly less alert.

As we gathered, I asked Eric how Goran fit into this. He smiled tiredly and said "Money. Money, and power."

Susan added, "If he can perfect the procedure to a point where the subjects don't know that they are being changed, to where they can be controlled and guided? His employers will reward him with far more than money. The leader of Sabre is putting it simply, a megalomaniac. Her ruling the world would be..." she paused a moment "bad on a grand scale".

On that cheery note, we got into the two armored SUVs the newcomers had brought.

Next stop MiracleLabs.

Chapter 13

- -

O
ur drive ended up being more interesting than I thought it would be. Susan drove, I was in the passenger seat while Gia, Calia, Rick, and Billy rode in the back seats.

As we drove, Susan casually asked, "Did Eric tell you guys that Shawn and I are different?"

I figured I knew what she was talking about, so I said "No, I just assumed you are like Eric and me. You know, turning into something between and alien and human, which is seriously disturbing, by the way."

"Oh." She said in the same tone my mom used to tell me that my hamster ate all of her babies, years ago.

"So, I'm not right about that?" I asked, even though I didn't want to hear the answer.

Susan sighed. "No, you aren't, but you need to know. Rick? You listening back there?"

Rick said "Yes, not napping back here!"

Susan glanced over at me and took a deep breath before continuing. "I need you all to promise not to lose your shit over this."

Rick and I said "Okay" in unison.

"Shawn and I, well, we transform." Her voice was carefully level and I think she was angry at Eric for leaving this to her.

Billy piped up suddenly. "You're a werewolf? Wow, I've never met another one before!" He sounded excited.

"Yeah, so I've heard. We'll be taking you to a place where you will receive training. After we're done tonight, of course."

I wondered again if this was just a long, vivid dream. Maybe I was in a coma, and this was what my brain had decided to fill my time with.

I knew that wasn't the case and it was unsettling. However, I was on my way to do something incredibly stupid that might get me killed, so silver lining, might not have to deal with it at all after tonight.

Compartmentalize, I told myself. Deal with it all later.

Meanwhile, Rick just sat there, mouth open, looking much less excited than he had been about the aliens. He turned his head slowly to look at Billy, then with obvious effort, shook his head and smiled.

"Okay. Got it. I wish my Nana was still alive because she would love being able to say I told you so to my mother." Rick was obviously compartmentalizing too. Or he had just given up and decided to roll with whatever happened and deal with it later like I had.

We slowed as we turned. We were approaching our destination. We had decided to park at an abandoned factory that was up a hill from the ML facility.

It was scheduled to be torn down, but for now, it was a place where we could put the vehicles out of sight. From the roof, we could get an idea of the outdoor patrol schedule and have a little time to check that everyone knew what they needed to do.

Trudging up three floors worth of stairs was a stark reminder that I had spent the last few months not doing a whole lot. I was winded by the time I reached the roof. A definite reminder to start going to the gym again if we lived through the night.

I had a terrible thought, so I went over to where Susan, Shawn, and Eric were clustered, deep in conversation.

"Um, Guys?" I started, feeling foolish for even having to bring this up. "So, if we've got psychics and werewolves, what are we likely to face in there? Are they likely to have the same?" As they turned toward me, I added, "By the way, it feels crazy to even have to say those words in that order."

Shawn said "Werebear."

I glared at Shawn and rolled my eyes. That was his only response to my question? Really?

Susan and Eric exchanged a look.

The other normal humans and I stared at them for a long time.

Finally, Susan spoke.

"We are likely to find some people with abilities like you and Eric. There are unlikely to be shifters, but there may be some who use... other means to fight." She faltered at the end.

"What other means?" Matt asked. He sounded angry. "I'm willing to do this, but I'm not up for walking in blind."

Susan nodded. "I understand, but I need you functional and some of this is hard to believe, hard to accept for most people."

"We passed that a long time ago." Matt answered with a snort. "I get it. You're afraid we're going to lose it, but right now? It's either real or it isn't. If it's real, denying it isn't useful, crying in a corner isn't any better, so we face it and deal with it later. I'd like to be alive when this is over, so I'll take anything you can give us about what might be in there."

We had aligned into three groups, Susan, Shawn, Billy, and Calia stood together. Matt, Gia, and Rick were the second cluster, while Eric and I stood between them.

There was an uncomfortable silence.

Finally, Eric looked at Susan. "You're sending them in blind if you don't tell them what you think is in there. Whatever your orders, I doubt getting these people killed is what you want."

Susan looked at us and exhaled.

"I'm not sure what might be in there, but you should be ready for anything. Remember I gave you special ammunition? The magazines are color coded. If I say blue, you reload with blue if I say yellow, reload with yellow. I am hoping we can get in and out without making contact, but if we do, it is imperative that you follow my instructions."

"You are likely to see some unbelievable things. Don't think too much about it. After this is over, we'll deal with any emotional or psychological fallout. Our employer is good at that." Shawn added. "We've come this far, don't you want to see how it ends?"

"Fine. But, since all this other shit is real, I will fucking haunt you if you get me or anyone else killed." Matt rubbed his face with his hands. Then he went to the edge of the roof and stood, watching the complex below.

We were all tired and on edge; adding more uncertainty wasn't a great idea, but nothing about this situation felt good.

I sat down, cross legged on the rooftop and began breathing slowly, concentrating on my heart rate. I couldn't change anything, but I could probably get a look inside.

I shut out the sounds of conversation around me, the murmur of the teams huddled around the tablet as Gia manipulated the drone. That wasn't for me right now. I needed to go inside.

I flew toward the large building. I could see the lit sign, but I didn't want the front of the building, I needed to go to the back door.

On my way to the back door, I passed two security guards riding in a golf cart. They didn't so much as glance toward me, which made sense, as I wasn't there.

I felt my mind wandering and pulled back to my task. My awareness of the people around me on the rooftop faded. The door was ahead of me, a light above it lighting the path. There was a small black bubble above the door, a camera.

I passed easily through the door, to find myself in a hallway that led left and right. The path to the left was short, ending in what looked like a breakroom. No visible camera in there, the two doors in the room led to a bathroom and a small closet.

The corridor right held several doors. Two were locker rooms, both empty, with signs for men and women. The next was a utility room, mops, brooms, and chemicals neatly put away, a chair with a paperback novel on the seat was evidence that someone used the room as a place to relax.

I saw no cameras in any of these spaces, though there was a single guard who came around the corner and walked down the hall. He entered each of the locker rooms and continued to the break room.

The corridor turned and I drifted through the closed double doors to a large open room. This space looked industrial, but a clean white version of it. None of the machinery was active, but it looked like a packing area, boxes sat in a labyrinth of shelves at one end of the space, the loading docks were probably beyond. Three guards patrolled this area, all armed, I noticed.

Someone might be able to get around their rotation with good timing.

Cameras here were abundant; they would cover most of the space. I pictured where each of them was so I could mark them on the blueprints later.

Across the room an open stairway led to the upper floor. As I drifted, I noticed that the industrial look of the lower floor gave way to a slightly nicer décor, traditional office space. There was beige carpeting, offices with doors and discreet cameras.

There were offices on this level, small with nameplates that indicated research staff worked two to an office. Two more guards in the offices, though these two looked bored out of their minds.

From the blueprints, I remembered I'd find the labs and cold storage on this level, past the offices.

Above would be the executive offices, I spied a staircase leading upward, again open with a rail on the upper floor. I could see a small sitting area from my vantage, along with at least one guard. I moved past the staircase and the nearby elevator to the next area on my agenda.

The labs were pristine, spotless, and looked as though no work was done there.

Nothing was out of place. The area designated by the blueprints as cold storage held empty shelves as I drifted inside.

There were no guards.

This was wrong. I was missing something.

I backtracked to the elevator. It was key operated, but I didn't need a key, because I had no body.

I followed the elevator shaft downward, to the bottom and flowed through the door. I was in a large, well lit, tidy, space. It was obviously in use regularly, very different from the perfectly organized rooms upstairs. Here I could see the human hand, a folder left on a chair, equipment not perfectly lined up, a notepad forgotten on a countertop.

As I drifted forward to check for cameras, I ran into a wall.

I looked around and saw nothing for a moment, then there was a flash of movement and a searing pain in my head.

I thought I heard laughter as I faded away.

I was back on the roof, lying on my back.

Calia was staring down at me.

"Are you all right?" She asked. "There was a ward."

I sat up. I had the mother of all migraines.

"Where are the others?" I asked.

"They are heading to their positions. You called out the camera locations as you viewed the area. Don't you remember that?" she asked tipping her head to the side.

"Um, no, I don't. I told you guys the locations. That's useful."

"Yes, it is. Would you like me to help you with your headache? You will need to go back in and watch the entry team." Calia's delivery was stilted, formal.

"If you can get rid of the headache, then yes, please."

She put her hands on my head, they were cool and soft. "Close your eyes and count to ten please."

I did and by the time I got to ten, the pain was gone and I was less tired than I had been a few seconds before.

I turned on my earpiece to find out what was happening with the other two teams.

"Hey, Calia. What did you mean by a ward?" I asked.

I stood up and looked toward the building. I couldn't see anyone, which expected. There was no chatter to be heard, also expected, so things were going well.

So far anyway.

"There was a ward against psychic intrusion. I do not believe it tracked you, it simply stopped your progress. Tracking such a thing is difficult and this ward was clumsy, poorly constructed." Her tone was matter of fact, as this was something I should understand in any way.

I was so far over my head that I was afraid I'd never come back. I was endangering my friends and some strangers on the say so of a guy I had met a couple of times for a group I knew nothing about.

Why? Because I felt it was important. In a way that felt real, something about this situation, the whole crazy, screwed up mess felt like a turning point.

If it was destiny or some such thing, I'd rather do anything else.

As I was running through my mental gymnastics, Calia touched my shoulder and gestured to a yoga mat someone had laid out on the rooftop. "I think you should lie down this time. It will be easier for you."

I lay down and closed my eyes. I felt like an idiot, because this was all so unbelievable and strange.

"Check on the guard house team first." Calia prompted. "I will be with you, watching and acting through your consciousness.

"Wait, what?" I sat back up.

"I cannot project as you do, however, I can work through your vision. It is difficult to explain, and we have little time. It will not harm you and may help significantly in completing our tasks. Concentrate on one of your friends."

I thought about Rick and suddenly, I was looking over his shoulder.

He was behind Gia, crouched in the darkness, moving toward the guard house at the main entrance.

One man sat inside, looking at a computer screen, his face illuminated by a bluish glow. Security cameras, placed at intervals along the path one would take to the front doors promised good coverage of the area.

Calia spoke a few words in a guttural language. A tiny shower of sparks emitted from each of the cameras. It looked like a chain reaction.

I heard another murmur next to me as Rick and Gia moved toward the guardhouse.

The guard was looking at his screen. I moved closer and looked over his shoulder. His screen was divided into eight small boxes, all black. The guard sighed and stepped outside to find Gia standing in front of him.

He reached for his shoulder mounted microphone, but Rick pulled him close with an arm around his throat before he could use it.

Gia whispered "Be quiet and you'll be OK. Do you understand?"

The guy nodded as best he could while being restrained, then, there was a whisper through my mind and he went limp in Rick's arms. Rick lowered him to the ground and secured his hands and feet with zip ties before stashing him under the desk.

I heard him mutter "What the hell?". Gia shrugged and gave the unconscious guard a last glance before they began to move toward the main building. Apparently they couldn't get into the security system from here.

That was probably Calia 'working through me'. I started to think about it and stopped as I felt my vision fading. Need to stay on task, I thought, no wandering attention.

I heard a whisper again. "You can move on the other team. Focus on one of them."

My point of view moved higher. I heard the faint whirr of the drone above as my vision flew over the top of the building.

I paused to look down at the roof. There was a helicopter. It hadn't been there before; I was almost sure. Surely someone would have said something about a helicopter.

I moved on, traveling toward Eric and Matt. Soon, I reached the corner of the building and saw them lined up.

Calia suggested that I stay with Matt, who was at the head of the group.

They were in the shadow of the building, then, with a few whispered words from Calia, they all but disappeared. I knew they were there, but they were bare outlines in the darkness.

They moved stealthily to the employee entrance I had gone through earlier. The door opened revealing a young woman with chin length black hair and square framed glasses wearing a white lab coat. She gestured at them to follow her.

I figured she must be the inside source.

Eric spoke to her as they stepped inside. They were visible again, no longer improbably transparent. Again, I guessed that Calia had something to do with that.

I reflected that once this was over, I was going to hide in my apartment under a blanket until I forgot everything that happened this week. In the back of my mind, I was still hoping this was a coma dream.

Of course, once my mind began to wander, everything around me dimmed, so I shut that down and tried to corral my errant thoughts.

Everything was going well. They team moved quickly and quietly down the hall behind the young woman who led them through the packing area, taking circuitous route to the staircase.

The red light on the camera at the top of the stairs disappeared in a shower of sparks, and they moved upward.

There were lights on in several offices, apparently some of the science staff worked late. Those lights hadn't been on when I was there earlier.

The place had been deserted except for the guards.

Wait, there were no guards inside the facility now. None.

They went up the stairs, crouched, nearly silent, and headed toward the elevator.

I moved my view and hovered right in front of Eric. He had seen me before. I felt panic rising and it was enough to nearly shake me out of whatever I was doing.

Eric finally stopped. He held up a hand and the group paused.

"Mara?" he asked, into my mind.

"YES! There is a helicopter on the roof and the guards are gone, there were guards before, but they aren't here!"

"Yes they are, we've avoided them." He answered through our link.

"No, they aren't here. I don't know what you are seeing, but I can't see them at all!"

Eric looked alarmed. He whispered, "We may be walking into a trap."

It must have gone out over their comms because everyone in the line tensed.

To me, he said...thought? "Anne says the lab we're looking for is in the basement."

"NO! There was a ward? Be careful."

I felt Calia near me and heard her say "I'll stay with you and disrupt the ward."

"Calia says she'll disrupt it. Are Rick and Gia coming to join you?"

"They are our backup, for if things go bad."

"Elevator, give me a few minutes."

I drifted down, to the bottom of the shaft.

Calia warned me to stay in the darkness once I got there. I felt an electric pulse in the air, heavy and oppressive like an approaching thunderstorm.

I hovered, waiting for a sign that it was time to move forward.

Finally, I felt a wave wash over me...it felt cool, a breeze after the storm.

I moved through the elevator door. Nothing stopped my movement, I glided through the tiny open area to the lab complex.

Dr. Goran leaned against a wall and waved at me as I entered. He could see me!

Behind him, were four large men in security uniforms. They didn't seem to see me.

I stopped.

The others would be coming down the elevator any moment.

I couldn't move. I seemed to be locked in place. I began to panic.

Dr. Goran came closer. He walked a slow circle around where I hovered, where my consciousness hovered?

His smile was filled with malice.

His voice was different than it had been in the hospital as he spoke in a calm, but resonant voice.

"Leave!"

Chapter 14

I sat up, gasping for breath.

A weight over my legs turned out to be Calia; she was out like a light.

I turned on my earpiece, but it must have been too far away, or the basement blocked the transmission.

I tried to go back in, but exhaustion and worry were obviously too much for me to overcome, at least without more practice.

Finally, I remembered that Rick and Gia weren't with the main group, so I tried calling them.

An eternity later, I heard Rick's tense whisper over the link. "What?"

"It's me, Mara. Rick, something is happening. It was a trap or maybe a setup. I don't know, but they're in the basement with something. Calia is out cold, and I can't go back in, you know, the way I did before."

"You still on the roof?"

"Yes. What do you think I should I do?"

Just as I thought he wasn't going to answer, Rick's voice came back over the link.

"Leave Calia there and meet us at the ground floor. We're going in."

I moved her onto the yoga mat and put my rolled-up jacket under her head. She was breathing, but she was limp and unresponsive. I hoped she would be okay and wished I had time to get her an ambulance.

Then, I got my vest, for all the good it would do, and the rest of my gear and ran down the stairs.

I hoped we could get there before something terrible happened.

Rick and Gia drove up in a golf cart, I settled onto the back seat, and we drove off toward the back entrance.

Halfway there, Gia changed direction and drove to the loading dock. When we stopped, she pulled herself up and pulled something out of her backpack.

While she fiddled with something by the door, I tried again to view the inside of the place. I was too agitated, too worried to get it work, so I turned back to see what was going on at the door.

Rick and Gia were looking at a tablet that showed a ghostly black and white image of the area right inside the door they had stuck a camera under. Nothing was visible except an unmoving forklift and some shelves filled with pallets of boxes.

Gia left Rick to pull the camera back while she went to work on the lock. It took her longer than usual, finally, there was a muted click, and she opened the door a few inches to peer in.

I fidgeted while she took her sweet time checking things out. I knew caution was necessary, but I was worried and didn't like not knowing what was happening.

Switching to the other team's channel didn't help. It was silent, no, not silent, there was static. At least I knew where we needed to go when we got inside.

Finally, she pushed the door open and held her finger to her lips.

Yes, quiet. I'm not an idiot.

Rick followed her and I brought up the rear. We stuck to the shadows and made it to the stairs up to the offices.

Still no movement.

I went toward the elevator, but Gia stopped me with a hand on my arm.

She looked at her tablet and led us past the elevator to the unused lab space. There, at the back of the room, was a door marked "Stairs".

We opened the door and began the process of going down the cement stairs quietly. Every noise was amplified by the open space, echoing. That didn't make the tension any less, but we eventually made it to the bottom.

Gia peeked through the tiny window and held her finger to her lips.

Quiet. Got it.

She eased through the door followed by Rick. I brought up the rear.

She and Rick both had their guns out. That didn't inspire confidence about whatever she saw through the window.

I quietly drew mine as well, hoping we were in time to make a difference.

We had come out between two doors marked "Men" and "Women". Bathrooms for this level. Another door stood between us and the main room.

It didn't have a window in it.

My heart pounded as I noticed that there was sound from behind the door, muted, but definite, and it wasn't conversation. Sounded like gunshots. Mostly.

Rick and Gia looked at each other and opened the door.

The three of us slipped out. The noise was louder, but we weren't at the source yet.

Another corridor, thirty or so feet long led to another door. This one had a window and even from the distance, we could see motion through it.

We moved quickly to the door, paused briefly to peer through the window and spilled out into chaos.

Two enormous furry forms were slashing at two of the security guards. They looked different than they had before, their skin appeared metallic, and they were holding their own with the...yeah, the werewolf and werebear better known as Susan and Shawn.

Matt and the others used desks as makeshift cover as they fired at the other two, but neither side appeared to be winning, at least not yet.

Dr. Goran was nowhere to be seen.

My two companions leapt into the fight, adding their firepower to the rest with the bonus of firing from a different direction.

I crouched near the door, trying to get a read on where we were. Eric sat behind one of the desks holding his right shoulder. He looked like he was in pain.

I stepped behind the door and sat on the floor where I'd be hidden if the door opened.

I tried one more time to center enough to reach out with my mind.

A loud roar shattered the seed of calm I had managed to find. I lurched to my feet and slammed the door open. Dr. Goran had rejoined the melee and he brought backup.

His backup was a huge creature, at least ten feet tall, long limbed and covered in stringy hair and tufts of fur. It looked angry as it grabbed Shawn and bit him in the shoulder. He roared and fought, but the creature kept hold of him.

Bullets flew in its direction, but they didn't seem to have much effect.

It threw Shawn against a wall as Susan leapt onto its back, sunk her claws in and began biting at the back of its neck.

I looked up and saw Dr. Goran standing, a smirk on his face. Bastard thought he had won this.

Thing about me is that if someone thinks they've won, I'll fight to the death to prove them wrong.

Again, not my best trait, but it has worked both for and against me in the past.

I glared at him and dropped behind the nearest desk.

Then, I forced my consciousness out of my body and headed straight for Goran.

He was distracted, watching the fight, so I had a second to take stock of him.

His eyes were wrong. Instead of dark brown, they glowed a deep burnished gold.

He wasn't aware of me, he was too intent on the fight, the fight that my friends were losing.

Susan went flying toward the wall and hit with a loud thud. She slid to the floor, leaving a wide streak of bright red behind. Her arm hung at an odd angle, but she looked up at the creature and howled. Shawn staggered to his feet as well and they attacked together.

Both security guards had stopped firing and were huddled behind desks.

I turned to Goran, who was watching the fight with obvious enjoyment. He stood in the open, without a care in the world.

I moved closer to him. What could I do to stop this?

I remembered Calia working through me. How it had felt, the sensation as power washed over me, and I gathered my thoughts. I imagined an icicle made of sheer force, air and what the hell, lightning. With no time for doubt or logic, I plunged it into the back of Dr. Goran's neck.

The world shattered around me, and everything went black.

Chapter 15

As I woke up, I listened to the sounds around me.

It was quiet. Peaceful.

The pillow under my head was lumpy, the mattress thin and uncomfortable. The air smelled of antiseptic.

It was all a dream. A vivid, terrible dream. The words "coma dream" came to mind.

I sighed and relaxed into the lumpy pillow and pulled the too-thin blanket up over me as I rolled over.

"Hey, you're awake!" It was Rick's voice.

I opened one eye and looked at him. "How long was I out?"

He wore a faded blue t-shirt and his hair was standing on end, probably due to his habit running his hand through it.

He looked happy to see me.

I opened the other eye and smiled back at him. I was happy to see him too.

"I had the weirdest dream. I had these psychic powers and we all got in this big fight. There was a werewolf named Susan and..." I trailed off when I saw the look on his face.

"Yeah, about that." He looked at me and took my hand in his.

"Not a dream?"

"Nope."

I squeezed his hand; he squeezed back.

"Good to see you. Let me get dressed and you can drive me home." I sat up. "How long have I been here this time?"

"Two days. You've been out for two days. I was worried."

I got a good look at him. His face was bruised, had a bandage on his forehead, and a brace around his other hand and wrist, the one not holding mine.

"How are you doing, Rick?" I asked, stunned by the realization that he had been hurt.

"I'm good. Bumps, bruises, and a sprained wrist. Give me a few days and I'll be my old self."

I was relieved. Rick had been beside me; I realized that I couldn't imagine life without him. Of course, I changed the subject.

"So, think they'll let me out today?"

He looked cornered. That could only mean one thing. He knew something that he didn't want to tell me.

I was just about to badger him until he told me when he was saved by the door. It opened and a young woman in white scrubs came in, carrying a clipboard.

"Oh, you're awake, good!" She set her clipboard down on the table beside my bed and began asking me a series of questions about how I felt.

I was fine, a little stiff, a little sore and curious about the bars on the one small window.

She didn't want to talk about the windows, so I went another direction.

"I'm feeling good. When can I get out of here?" I kept my voice cheerful and my eyes wide open to appear friendly and engaged.

Based on Rick's expression I did not nail it.

The nurse said "Not today. The doctor will be in to speak with you shortly. Your visitor will need to leave. Mr. Garcia, don't you have somewhere else you need to be?"

Rick got up, leaned over, and whispered "Behave." Then he left.

"Which doctor? Not Doctor Goran?" I felt a stab of fear as I re-called the last thing I'd seen.

"No. Doctor Sanderson will be coming to see to you. She'll escort you to your first therapy session."

"Therapy session?" I was genuinely confused. I don't need therapy; I need to get out of here and sleep in my own bed."

"I understand that you may not be entirely comfortable with this, but it is something you will need to do. If you cooperate, things will go much more smoothly."

"What hospital is this?" I asked.

The nurse sighed. "I can't share that information at this time."

"Why?"

She ignored my question in favor of wrapping a blood pressure cuff around my arm. After blood pressure, she took my temperature, and listened to me breathe.

I was about to start asking questions again, when a white-haired woman in a white coat came in. The sight of the white coat filled me with anxiety, so I began breathing slowly and deliberately to calm myself.

The nametag on her coat read "Dr. Sanderson". She was small, gray haired, and would have been grandmotherly if not for the frown on her face. She didn't look friendly at all.

She pulled up the chair Rick vacated and stared at me with piercing blue eyes.

"So, Miss Ryan, tell me about your remote viewing capabilities."

"My what?"

"Remote. Viewing. Capabilities. What can you tell me about the times when your body is in one place, and you can see another as if you were physically there?" Her tone was clipped, impatient.

"What makes you think I can do that?"

"Don't think me a fool, young lady." She was definitely impatient. "Answer the question."

"Um, I don't know. It feels like I'm invisible or something. It's hard to describe. How do you know about it? Did Eric tell you?"

She changed topics again. "Your vitals are all good. As you are recovering well, please put your shoes on and come with me. It is time for your RRT group. You will attend daily until such time as we feel that you are ready to leave this facility."

"Wait, am I a prisoner?" I asked starting to get angry. I felt a buzzing in my head, like static electricity.

Another voice interrupted. This one I was recognized.

"Margaret. Stop. I'll take her to group." It was Susan. She looked a lot less rough than Rick, but last time I saw her she was badly injured.

Dr. Sanderson and Susan stared each other down for a moment. I got the impression they weren't particularly fond of each other.

The doctor left and Susan grabbed a pair of slippers from under the bed. "Here, put these on. You want a robe or are the scrubs okay?"

I looked down and realized I was dressed in light purple scrubs. "At least my butt won't be hanging out for all the world to see. These are way better than a hospital gown." I stepped into the slippers. "So, what happened after I, um, passed out?"

"A lot. You saved us. Most of us. Three of the four security guards from the facility died when Goran lost control of the troll. Except it wasn't really Goran. He- . "

"The what?" I interrupted, incredulous.

"The troll. They had it in one of the labs. Troll blood was an ingredient in their anti-aging cream. It works, but harvesting it makes the troll extra angry." She chuckled. "Goran lost control when you stabbed him. People here are still trying to figure out how you did that."

She continued as we walked down the hallway. "Me? I don't care. We lived. Shawn is still recovering, Gia has a concussion, Eric took a bullet in an arm, but they're both going to be fine. Matt, if you can believe it, came through without a scratch."

"What about Calia?" I asked, remembering how pale she was lying on the roof.

"She's fine. She'll need a few weeks of quiet and rest, but she's tougher than she looks. She really liked working with you."

We arrived at a set of double doors. Beyond, I saw a circle of chairs and a few people moving around. A man in a white coat sipped a cup of coffee near a table where I also spotted snacks.

"Goran's eyes were wrong. The color, the way he moved..." I trailed off, not sure how to describe it.

Susan put her hand on my shoulder. "Dr. Goran wasn't himself for a good long time."

She took a deep breath. "There is a whole world underneath what most people see. You have experienced a small part of that. That's why you're here. You can't unsee things or stop knowing them. So, we'll help you integrate that knowledge into your life. Hopefully, you'll be willing to work with us when we need you or you need us."

She impulsively hugged me. "I remember how scared I was at first. It's a lot to take in. Now, go. Doctor Hill is a good guy. Look, Rick is already there; I think he saved you a seat."

I turned and walked to the circle and sat down next to Rick. He handed me a cardboard cup of coffee and a muffin. The man knows what I like and what I need.

Dr. Hill stood and looked around the circle. "I see we have a new-comer. Welcome to Reality Realignment Therapy".